THE FIRST CHURCH ON THE MOON

The First Church on the Moon

By JMR Higgs

the big hand

Published by The Big Hand

First print edition 2013

Text © JMR Higgs 2013
Cover design by JMR Higgs, images by iStockphoto

www.bighandbooks.com
www.johnhiggs.com
www.facebook.com/johnhiggsauthor

ISBN 978-0-9564163-3-9

The following takes place 160 years after the events in *The Brandy of the Damned*.

By the same author:

FICTION
The Brandy of the Damned (The Big Hand, 2012)

NON-FICTION
I Have America Surrounded: The Life of Timothy Leary (The Friday Project, 2006)

NEITHER FICTION NOR NON-FICTION
The KLF: Chaos, Magic and the Band who Burned a Million Pounds (Phoenix, 2013)

1.

Jennifer Hammerpot, the Agnostic Bishop of Southwark, looked at the moon buggy with suspicion.

Marcus Milk, a jilted groom, looked at the floor and made involuntary whimpering noises. He was still dressed in the suit he wore for his abandoned wedding the previous day.

Gregor Milk, Commander of the Steve Moore Moonbase at the lunar south pole, looked thoughtfully at Bishop Hammerpot, then at his son Marcus, and finally at the medical notes about his son that he held in his hand.

The moon buggy looked like crap.

'Are there no other vehicles?' asked Bishop Hammerpot. It was the only transport remaining in the large, echoing moonbase hanger, but something about its dust-caked shell made her uneasy. Its presence made her mind play ominous music. It looked like a drawing of a moon buggy by a left-handed child at a Victorian school where they beat pupils who don't use their right hands were beaten.

Gregor rubbed his chin. He had a good chin, solid and stubbly, and he liked to spend a good proportion of his working day stroking it. He turned to Bishop Hammerpot, but he ignored her question. "You're trying to tell me that these people from America... what were they called?" he said.

"Americans."

"Americans, right. You think that these 'Americans' flew to the moon?"

Jennifer nodded, but she did so cautiously. "I think it's possible," she said.

"In the twentieth century?" continued Gregor.

"Yes. In 1969."

"Before computers and airplanes?"

"Er... before modern computers, yes, but after airplanes. About 25 years after the invention of the jet engine."

"So just after they invented planes and before they invented computers, some 'Americans' might have flown to the moon. That's what you're saying?"

Jennifer nodded, a little embarrassed.

"It doesn't sound very likely, Bishop."

"I know, but hear me out. I've spent most of my life studying the twentieth century. There is evidence that points to this. It's circumstantial, yes, and the sources are poor, but it's consistent. I know it sounds impossible and I admit it's unlikely, but if it happened there will be evidence, and that evidence could save us all. And I know where it would be."

"Go on," said Commander Milk, against his better judgement.

"The stories say that they landed near the Sea of Tranquillity."

Gregor winced. The Bishop's plan was getting more implausible by the second. The Sea of Tranquillity was on the trademarked side of the moon.

Marcus made a small sobbing noise from somewhere underneath his limp fringe. It was the sort of noise you don't expect to hear from men in their late twenties. Jennifer and Gregor pretended not to notice.

The Bishop stepped closer to the Commander and adopted her most reasonable and persuasive voice. She had decided to play the Bishop card. If that didn't work, she'd just look up at him with her big green eyes, which was always a good Plan B.

"I'm not asking you to believe this, just to recognise that I think it's possible. No-one would blame you for accepting the advice of a bishop. Let me have the buggy. If I don't find anything, then what have you lost?" She paused for effect and then added, "And what other options do you have?"

Gregor Milk looked down at the medical notes in his hand, then over at his son. He rubbed his mighty chin once more, then shook his head. Despite Jennifer's textbook playing of the Bishop card, the idea that their lives would be saved by proving the moon was visited in 1969 had entirely been rejected by his neurons.

"Sorry Bishop, but the answer is 'no'. That's a fool's errand, and I have need of you here. I want you to look after my son. Find out what's wrong with him. He was fine yesterday, when he was getting ready for his wedding, and now he's all floppy and groany and stuff." He handed her the medical notes.

"Don't waste my time again," he added, a touch harshly.

Gregor turned, his rubber soles squeaking on the plastic floor, and left the room to locate some coffee. His son looked up from the floor in time to watch him go.

Human brains are inherently lazy. Once they are set up to believe something they much prefer to go on believing it, rather than instigating all of the spawning of new synapses and general rewiring needed in order to believe something different. This is especially true if you ask them to turn a concept previously believed to be absurd into one that appears reasonable.

Unfortunately for Bishop Hammerpot, Gregor did not, at that time, have that amount of brain activity to spare. His brain was otherwise occupied.

Here is a breakdown of the mental activity occurring in Gregor Milk's head during his conversation with Bishop Hammerpot:

- Dealing with hangover (58.7% of brain capacity)
- Speaking, standing, looking in control, etc. (13%)
- Concern for son's strange affliction (8.6%)
- The imminent ending of life support shipments from the Earth, resulting in death of everyone on the moon (7%)
- Trying to piece together exactly what happened the night before (4.2%)
- Miscellaneous bureaucracy (3.9%)
- Coffee (1.7%)
- Nagging suspicion that history will remember him as a mutineer (1%)
- Other (1.9%)

Asking someone to believe one thing about the world when they are happy believing something else is always tricky. Much depends on the scale of the idea, and how important to their sense of identity that idea is. Convincing someone who believes that they left their keys in the pub that their keys are in fact in the dish by the TV is, in the grand scale of things, an achievable goal. Convincing the same person that both their parents are goats and therefore they themselves are a goat, albeit a clever and well-dressed one, is considerably more challenging. Likewise, convincing the average person in the year 2171 that 'Americans' had gone to the moon in 1969 is ambitious, especially if that person is a hungover moonbase commander.

Bishop Hammerpot watched Commander Milk walk away. If she had been the sort of person who gave up easily, this would have been the end of the matter.

Bishop Hammerpot was not the sort of person who gave up easily.

2.

This is a story about events which occurred in the year 2171 CE. At that time not a lot was known about the twentieth century. The reason for this was the Great Backup Catastrophe of 2048, one of the blackest and most appalling days in human history.

By the mid-twenty first century, all culture, entertainment and information was digital. There were simply too many songs, movies and books, and it was no longer feasible to create actual physical versions of them all to put on shelves somewhere. Historians, artists and scientists had generated so much data that people began to feel physically sick just thinking about it.

People had no need to keep local copies of their data because it could all be accessed anywhere from any device connected to what was then called 'the cloud'. The cloud was a seemingly infinite, fast and above all cheap chunk of virtual online storage. It was a good system, even if it did lead to mass redundancies amongst the ranks of shelving manufacturers.

Unfortunately, there was a reason why the cloud was so cheap. The data was physically stored at giant server farms in the country then known as the United States of America. This data needed to be backed up, in case of fire, earthquake, hen party or other natural disaster. The job of backing up the data was outsourced to a company in China. The Chinese company found that it made financial sense to take on the contract whilst outsourcing the actual backing-up work to a company in Western Africa. The Africans, in turn, outsourced the task to an Australian company who had given them a really amazingly cheap quote. The Australian company was able to store the data so cheaply because all they were doing was taking that data, sticking it in a giant archive marked 'BACKUP – DO NOT DELETE', and simply copying that back onto the cloud.

So it was that, on the fateful day when a sudden excess of scandal and outrage caused the internet to explode and the cloud to wipe itself in a fit of hysteria, the technical people in charge of these things went looking for the backup in order to rebuild the internet and discovered that they didn't have one. The whole of the world's data was lost to posterity.

That was an awkward phone call.

Humanity has never really recovered from the Great Backup Catastrophe of 2048 CE. Profound despair spread across the more middle-class areas of the world. Financial markets descended into anarchy, as usual, but this was a higher level of anarchy than their normal level of anarchy. People struggled to remember the names of their extended families, mortgage lenders or what that actor had been in before. Commentators at the time likened the loss of human culture to the burning of the Great Library of Alexandria. They then went to Wikipedia to look up a few more details about the burning of the Great Library of Alexandria, found that it was blank, and went mad with horror.

Humanity recovered, to an extent, but most human knowledge was lost for good. The result of this tragedy was that the true history and culture of the twentieth century became largely unknown.

A major academic exploration into twentieth century America did occur, following the discovery in 2089 of hundreds of surviving VHS cassettes. Each one of these contained an example of something called a 'Hollywood action movie' from circa 1980. A video recorder was reverse engineered by some particularly keen honour students, allowing teams of academics to watch and study these precious historical recordings. After years of intense and scholarly debate, a consensus arose that the videos were probably drug-induced, intended for a ritual purpose, and that the traditional notion of a 'United States of America' was a fictional conceit much like Atlantis or Narnia.

The notion that 'Americans' flew to the moon in the year 1969, therefore, was not something that Bishop Hammerpot would find it easy to convince anyone of.

3.

Commander Milk marched decisively through the winding moonbase corridors, entered the crew room, and poured himself a cup of black coffee. He held the cup up to near-shoulder height in an impressively decisive manner. He was very good at acting decisively and always did so whenever he had no idea what to do.

He took a swig from the cup and turned to look firmly at one wall, and then another, before quickly exiting the room and marching towards his quarters. The room was empty and his display of purposefulness was therefore pointless, but he performed it out of habit and it made him feel a little better.

Most of Gregor's career success was due to his ability to appear decisive in front of his co-workers. All workers understand that a decisive manager means trouble. Should you approach a decisive manager with a problem they will immediately designate a course of action which, due to their lack of consideration or insight into the nuances of the situation, will make things many times worse. Workers with managers like this quickly learn that it is better to solve any problem themselves. They have no choice, therefore, but to go about their business in a conscientious, hardworking manner. It is for this reason that useless but decisive people get promoted into management positions.

Gregor walked purposefully into his quarters and, when the door had closed behind him, fell onto his bed, curled himself into a ball and put the pillow over his head.

Twenty minutes later he was disturbed by a beep. It was a message from Azimuth, his senior IT analyst, who wanted the Commander to join him in the engineering labs as soon as possible.

Gregor went back under his pillow and counted down from thirty. Then he stood up, regained the posture of a commander brimming with purpose and certainty, and marched out of his quarters.

The Steve Moore Moonbase was nestled in the depths of the Shackleton crater, at the moon's South Pole. It was built in the shape of a duck. Many people wondered why the moonbase was built in the shape of a duck, but every single person who researched the matter found the answer terribly disappointing. It was much better not to know.

Engineering was at the far end of the base, in the area known as the Duck's Head. Gregor was dimly aware of encountering an almost total lack of crew as he strode towards engineering. He had never known the base to be so quiet, or the corridors to be so littered with spilt Bombay Mix and discarded items of clothing. Had he not been striding with such authority, he may have been tempted to stop and think about this. He may also have noticed Bishop Hammerpot, who peeped out of her quarters after he had passed and tiptoed away in the general direction of the stores.

Gregor arrived in Engineering and was immediately pointed towards a bank of computer screens by a noticeably twitchy Azimuth. Azimuth had an unusual appearance because the dark hair of his beard was considerably curlier than the hair on his head, and that's just wrong. He also hadn't slept in four days, but this was normal and largely a result of his forgetfulness.

Azimuth started to speak but Gregor silenced him with a raised finger. Azimuth was forced to wait while Gregor pretended to absorb the display of information before him.

"Dennis," barked Gregor at the banks of computers, "Can you model a scenario which does not lead to the deaths of everyone on the base?"

Dennis was the name given to the virtual verbal interface that sat above all the moonbase's computer systems. "No", he replied.

Gregor nodded.

"You asked me that a few hours ago," Dennis pointed out.

Gregor ignored him and turned his attention to Azimuth, who was attempting to steer his attention towards a box of code on a screen.

"Commander, I think I know what's happened with the Turtles but I will need your clearance level to disable it. If you would log on here..."

"Why do you need my clearance level?"

"Because you switched on the thing I need to switch off."

"Did I?"

"Yes sir, at 11:34 last Thursday."

Gregor thought back to last Thursday. He had been asked to do something computery around then, although he wasn't entirely sure what. He nodded decisively, then moved to the keyboard.

"And this will enable us to switch off the mobile light trucks, will it?"

"I think so, yes."

That was enough for Gregor. He entered his code.

Mobile light trucks, or 'Turtles' as they are commonly known, are a form of all-purpose automated mining equipment which were normally found trundling slowly through the dust on the dark side of the moon. They were bulky, squat vehicles which resemble giant upturned pigsties on fat tractor wheels. They were painted orange with red stripes. This may at first appear to be a questionable aesthetic direction, but you need to factor in the extent with which people on the moon are sick to the back teeth of anything grey.

The trucks were able to drill, survey and strip away the regolith which makes up the top layer of the moon's surface. They made a right mess of the place, basically. It was for this reason that there were restrictions preventing them from journeying to the earth-facing side of the moon. This near side was heavily trademarked by the YayM00n! Corporation, and any changes to it visible from the Earth would trigger colossal lawsuits.

The far side of the moon was in the public domain, and as such Commander Milk was free to mine the living bejesus out of it. Nobody on Earth could see the changes occurring on that side of the moon, which was just as well, because it now resembled a cross between a teenager's bedroom and a teenager's chin.

Mobile light trucks also carried a large energy transfer unit known, unimaginatively, as a 'light'. This device was normally used to transfer the staggering amounts of power generated on the moon across the 384,000km of empty space to the Earth. It did this by converting energy to very high frequency ultra-violet wavelengths and beaming these at a series of relay satellites, which safely and efficiently transfer that energy to whomever had the cash to pay for it. The device was also capable of producing regular light, of the type of wavelength which the human eye could detect. This function was rarely used because any human eye looking at this light was instantly fried into a form of shrivelled brown raisin.

Since the previous Thursday a number of these mobile light trucks had been leaving their regular working positions and embarking on the long journey over to the trademarked side of the moon. The reason Gregor had been persuaded to override the safeguards which normally prohibit such a journey was a wedding. This was not just any wedding. It was the first wedding on the moon.

The bride and groom for the first wedding on the moon were Gregor's son Marcus and Nathalie Grindles, an easy going and immensely likeable mineral analyst who had arrived on the moon six months earlier. The wedding was a big deal. An Agnostic Bishop had been dispatched from Earth to perform the ceremony. Tabloid news sites had gone crazy for the story, partly because of the romance, partly because of the novelty of it all, and partly because the moon's low gravity meant that women's breasts look great in photographs.

To recognise the Earth's interest in the ceremony, and to celebrate his son's big day, Commander Milk had been persuaded to make a highly irregular gesture. He had allowed twelve mobile light trucks to journey on to the trademarked side of the moon and position themselves in the shape of an immense heart, 400km across. At the finale of the ceremony they would turn on their light units, which would be set to a visible wavelength and directed at the Earth itself. The result, which would have been visible to the entire population of Europe, Asia and Africa, would be twelve lights appearing in the centre of the moon in the shape of a heart.

All this broke many laws, but it was also quite lovely, so Gregor thought he would get away with it.

Unfortunately the day of the wedding had not gone to plan.

Somehow it wasn't just twelve trucks that had journeyed to the earth-facing side of the moon, but the entire fleet of one hundred and eleven vehicles. These vehicles had not positioned themselves to make a heart: they had positioned themselves to spell out a message. It was this message that Azimuth was desperately trying to switch off, even as his hangover made every movement unacceptably painful.

The message formed by the Mobile Light Trucks read, *'Piss off Earth!'*

Once Gregor had entered the override code Azimuth began hammering at the system. With admirable efficiency for a man who should logically have been unconscious, he instructed every single vehicle to switch off its light and return to base. He then slid off his seat and curled up into a ball underneath his desk.

Gregor checked the screens. The message *'Piss off Earth!'* was no longer being displayed across the surface of the moon. This, he decided, was a good thing.

"Remind me, Dennis, who was with me last Thursday at 11:34?" he asked.

"Chief Maintenance Officer Orlando Monk," the software replied. Gregor nodded. It was coming back to him now.

"Instruct Security Officer Hoops to place Monk under arrest," said Gregor. He had always wanted to give an order like that, and it proved to be just as much fun as he always thought it would. It was a shame that the only crew member to witness it was underneath a desk and not paying attention.

"He may well be in bed, Commander, most people are," Dennis replied.

"Wake him up!"

Dennis paused for a fraction of a second longer than computer voices are supposed to pause. "I'll give it a go," he said.

"And call an emergency conference of all upper management level staff, to be held in the conference hall immediately," Gregor said. He was really on a roll now.

"All upper management level staff have gone back to bed, Commander."

Gregor was about to order the computer to wake them all when it occurred to him that at least one of his eyes was not working properly. He paused to think about this. This course of action proved informative, because he discovered that thinking caused his head to cramp. He also discovered that his nervous system had initiated something which the military would categorise as a 'blue-on-blue incident'.

"Dennis, I may go back to bed myself."

"Yes, Commander."

"Not for long, you understand."

"Yes, Commander."

"Monitor me. The moment I wake, call an immediate emergency conference of all upper management level staff. I don't care who you have to wake."

"Yes, Commander."

Gregor turned sharply and half-walked, half-crawled his way back across the duck-shaped moonbase.

4.

Security Officer Arnopp Hoops was not in bed. He was guarding the cat.

He didn't mind. It wasn't the most exciting of jobs, but he had no doubt that it was vitally important. Deep down Hoops would have preferred to have been doing something adventurous, such as chasing villains across the universe in state of the art spaceships, but guarding the cat was still quite good. In his younger days he had kept a file of stories about off-world military heroics, and he endlessly re-read accounts of particularly dangerous and thrilling escapades. But if he was honest, he didn't really want to be involved in such frightening events himself. He wasn't crazy. He would be happier just meeting those brave men, hanging out with them, and becoming their friend.

The cat's name was Bishmillah. She was large black cat with flecks of grey in its fur. She was not fat, exactly, but she was longer than what would normally be considered a reasonable length for a cat. She lay stretched out across the surface of a tumble drier in the laundry. She raised her head, opened her jaws wide, and yawned. Then she lay her head back on her paws and continued to doze.

Hoops watched her, like the professional he was.

This is not a subject that many people are comfortable talking about, but sometimes it needs to be said: some cats aren't very nice.

Most cats are fine, that goes without saying. Some are lovely. But some are miserable charmless sods, and Bishmillah was one of those cats. She didn't come up to you when you were tired to give you some affection. She didn't purr or meow, or like to have her tummy tickled. She just made horrible yowling noises when she wanted to be fed. Then she would wait for someone to fill her bowl, and then walk away and leave it uneaten. Occasionally she would bite people on the ankles or scratch any faces she took a dislike to.

Most of the time she slept. During those rare times when she was awake, she liked to chew through the cables of any machine that had an important role to play in moonbase life support. It was for this reason that Hoops was assigned the mission of guarding the cat, and ensuring that she didn't chew through anything important.

The cat didn't know it, but she was partly responsible for the romance between Marcus Milk and Nathalie Grindles. Marcus had brought the cat with him when he had arrived on the moonbase. No-one had ever brought a cat to the moon before because, in truth, it was a dumb thing to do. There were no cat spacesuits, so she was unable to go outside and get up to cat business. There were no mice to catch, or birds to watch, or walls to sit on. There was just miles and miles of vitally important cabling that was coated in a strange flexible plastic which felt quite interesting to the inside of a cat's mouth.

No-one told Marcus that bringing a cat to the moon wasn't a good idea, because he was the Commander's son and it seemed sensible to be nice to him. No-one told him how unlikeable the cat was either. As far as Marcus was concerned, when he brought Bishmillah to the moon he had done a good thing.

One of the first things that Nathalie noticed about Marcus was that he genuinely seemed to think that Bishmillah was a lovely cat. It didn't matter what she chewed through, or who she scratched, or which equipment she pissed in, he always managed to interpret her behaviour in a positive light. Even though every other member of the lunar colony had a strong dislike of the cat, which they would voice stridently when Marcus wasn't in ear shot, he remained ignorantly resolute in his opinion that Bishmallah was brilliant, and that everyone knew it.

Nathalie thought a lot about this aspect of Marcus. On one hand he was blatantly wrong, and therefore a terrible fool. Yet as faults go, blindly thinking the best of someone wasn't the worst. It was the sort of fault, she thought, that she could probably put up with in a partner.

Marcus was a little bit too handsome for her tastes. His features were exactly the right proportions and in exactly the right place. She had been worried that she would soon become bored of the sight of him, for there was nothing interesting about his features which her mind could snag onto. Yet his terrible failure of judgement might just compensate for that. Blind unflagging adoration could well be the thing which kept him interesting.

These were the thoughts which, one happy day, persuaded Nathalie Grindles to drop to one knee and perform the first proposal on the moon.

Arnopp Hoops watched the cat. He would have continued to watch her for a number of hours, if Azimuth hadn't buzzed and ordered him to go and arrest Orlando Monk.

Hoops couldn't believe his luck. He would have skipped out of the laundry immediately if he had not been so conscientious about his previous mission.

Hoops knew that if he ran off to do some good arresting there would be nothing to stop Bishmillah from having a good chomp on the cables of her choice. To prevent this he picked her up and placed her inside a tumble drier. This might have appeared cruel, but Hoops was acting for the greater good. He knew that there was no danger of asphyxiation inside one of those machines, and he unplugged it from the wall socket to prevent anyone switching it on by mistake.

Putting the cat inside the tumble drier was an act that didn't trouble Hoops' conscience, partly because he knew he would come and let her out again as soon as he could, but mainly because he didn't like her very much. Ignoring Bishmillah's unappealing squawks, he closed the tumble drier's door and dashed off to try his hand at some real security work.

5.

Bishop Hammerpot looked around the store room and tried to make sense of the filing system. She knew that she needed oxygen, hydrogen fuel tanks, water and something nice to eat, so she set about finding them.

The room was long, largely underground and smelt of fish. The quartermaster had long since given up trying to understand exactly why the room smelt of fish and had decided to embrace the phenomenon. A sign above the door read, 'Stores. First place on the moon to smell of fish.'

This may initially appear to be an historic milestone in the story of mankind but it should be understood in the context that, as the first permanent working community on the moon, the staff of the moonbase generated an awful lot of 'firsts'. Engineer Ravi Shropshire, for example, was the first person to cheat at poker on the moon. Technician Sally O'Allways was the first person to accidentally call a senior officer 'Dad' on the moon. Software Wrangler Mogadon Li was the first person to shit himself on the moon. He was strangely proud of this.

Of greater relevance were the recent actions of Chef Lark. In the past week Chef Lark had become the first person to successfully distil alcohol on the moon, a heroic achievement he dedicated to the wedding of Marcus Milk and Nathalie Grindles. Or, to be more accurate, a heroic achievement he dedicated to their post-wedding celebrations.

Alcohol had been forbidden throughout much of the history of mankind's presence on the moon. This prohibition dated back to an early voyage by a private expedition of wealthy geologists, who took a few bottles of champagne along for the ride. Upon arriving, and on confirmation that they were in the vicinity of unusually iron-rich forms of basalt, the geologists felt the urge to celebrate. In the absence of survivors it is not easy to say exactly what happened. Whether the excitement got the better of them or whether the effects of alcohol are more potent in low gravity has been much debated, but the fact remains that those little geology hammers can do a lot of damage. Taking alcohol to the moon was clearly not worth the risk.

For the early moon explorers, this prohibition was not controversial. The simple fact that they were actually standing on the moon was a giddy thrill in itself. It was an experience that they wished to remember for the rest of their days, and getting lashed as well would have been overkill. The situation changed with the establishment of the first permanent working moonbase. For the first time, people on the moon became bored. They were bored with the black sky and the grey landscape. They were bored of sweeping away the fine grey dust that, despite all their efforts, got everywhere. They were bored with messages from home that always started with the cheese joke.

More than anything, they were bored with craters. Craters were rubbish. They were everywhere, and they did nothing. After six months of nothing but craters, staff would develop a deep and profound understanding of just how brilliant trees were.

When Chef Lark began stockpiling sugars and began work on building a distillery, therefore, he received nothing but encouragement.

The result, known predictably as Chef Lark's Moonshine, was declared ready on the eve of the wedding. Strictly speaking it should have had another few weeks in the still to reach basic human consumption standards, but this wasn't really an option. In many ways, it was a miracle that it lasted as long as it did. During the final days the still had needed to be guarded by three strong miners and a cattle prod.

Bishop Hammerpot had not drunken copiously of Chef Lark's Moonshine. As a result she was one of the few people currently able to walk and think at the same time. This was partly because she had been on duty, and partly because as a small woman, at 5'2", she had a physical disadvantage in dealing with the marauding scrum around the bar.

A third factor was that the Bishop had attended the annual pan-European inter-faith summit before flying to the moon. It had been sponsored by a schnapps producer and a number of her organs were still in the process of self-repair.

Bishop Hammerpot diligently piled the supplies she needed on to a trolley, aided enormously by the low gravity and a basic ignorance of the quantities she required. She then pushed the trolley out along the deserted white moonbase corridors towards Marcus Milk's quarters. She had failed to persuade the Commander that their only hope was for her to journey to the Sea of Tranquillity and search for the landing section of a mythical ancient spacecraft known as the Apollo Eagle Lander. Her response to this was to embark on that quest without permission.

She had promised Milk that she would look after his son. As a Bishop she had no choice but to honour that promise, which meant that Marcus would have to go with her. This was no time to abandon her religious commitments. Plus, she didn't know how to drive a moon buggy, so taking Marcus along would work out quite well.

6.

The minds of citizens from 2171 CE saw the world around them very differently to people from earlier ages.

This in itself should not be surprising: mankind had evolved from scampering vole-like critters and clearly our consciousness had progressed along the way. The actions of our Stone Age ancestors, for example, could only be understood if we recognised that their minds had evolved to a level similar to that of dogs. True, they could talk and they maintained a stubborn obsession with magic rocks, but in terms of their everyday actions and their approach to life, they were basically canine. Likewise the great wars and dynastic squabbles of the Middle Ages made sense only once you realised that the medieval mind had evolved roughly to the level of a 12 year old boy. The twenty-first century showed that mankind had mentally evolved to the point of a forty year old accountant on the verge of a mid-life crisis.

The evolution of human consciousness is the defining aspect of history, so if we wish to understand the twenty second century it is necessary to recognise that, unlike earlier ages, the population had outgrown the concept of free will. The roots of this change go back to the late twenty first century and a great scandal involving the then King of England, Leslie the First.

For the first decade of his reign, King Leslie of England was a popular monarch. He was handsome, statesmanlike, and had the rare skill of wearing a crown in such a way that didn't look camp. It was something of a shock, therefore, when he absentmindedly butchered the daughter of the Icelandic President with a steak knife during a live global media broadcast.

As is well known, a life of untold wealth and constant reverence takes a psychological toll. The pampered children of the elite were given everything and earned nothing, so there was a tendency for them to find that their pleasures eventually left them jaded. For this reason it was long understood in royal circles that the monarchy must be allowed to indulge their desires to quite extreme degrees, if only to give them a reason to get out of bed in the morning.

Most English monarchs committed the occasional murder in order to stave off the crushing ennui. Queen Victoria liked to use an axe, George IV once ate a Dutchman and King Charles III used to hunt midwives. All this was considered inevitable and was routinely hushed up. King Leslie was no more bloodthirsty than most of his ancestors, but he was the first to indulge himself in public view. He had been bored out of his mind, unfortunately, and completely forgot where he was.

The public reaction was almost entirely negative, particularly in Iceland. A global mega-scandal of unimaginable proportions erupted. It is hard, for those not alive at the time, to appreciate the size of the scandal. There had been nothing like it beforehand and there will probably be nothing like it again. Historians refer to it as the 'Great Scandal' because the phrase 'mind-blowing holy shitstorm' is not considered to be rigorously academic.

King Leslie immediately issued a statement in order to limit the damage. He stressed that he was very sorry for his actions, offered his sympathy to the family of whoever it was who had been unlucky enough to be sitting next to him at the time, and hoped that we could all learn from the unfortunate incident and move on. This statement was also received negatively, and a number of media commentators came dangerously close to spontaneously bursting into flames.

The uproar soon produced two bitterly opposed camps, those who thought Leslie needed to be thrown into a dungeon for the rest of his life, and those who thought he should be hung at dawn. This dangerous impasse gave Leslie time to gather a crack team of lawyers to look into options for his defence. He stressed to them that he really was in favour of the 'saying sorry and moving on' option.

The lawyers looked into the situation and saw that the case was indeed a tricky one. The murder had been witnessed live by 6% of the global population and in recorded form by a further 83%. This made it difficult to deny the incident happened, or to frame an Irishman.

Analysis of the footage did not favour a plea of self-defence or give credence to the notion that she was "asking for it." With Iceland spearheading intense international pressure and the Metropolitan Police on the verge of calling in air strikes to control the mob outside Buckingham Palace, the lawyers returned to the King and informed him that he was basically fucked.

All the lawyers, that is, except one.

That lawyer was called Harrison Ford (not to be confused with the twentieth century actor of the same name). Ford was nearing retirement age. He had devoted his life to law and, if he was honest, he had not enjoyed any of it. The problem, as he saw it, was lawyers. Ford had been surrounded by lawyers his whole life and he had not liked them. As he grew older and more bad tempered he realised that what he would enjoy more than anything else was sticking it to the lot of them. For this reason he approached King Leslie and told him of what is known in legal circles as the 'nuclear option'.

The nuclear option was this: the entire body of criminal law rests on the existence of free will, yet the physical sciences have by and large shown that there is no such thing. Should the King be tried for his crimes and plead not guilty on grounds of the non-existence of free will, he would (a) have a strong case, and (b) bring about the total collapse of the entire legal profession.

Leslie found much to admire in this approach. He knighted Ford in a fit of enthusiasm and relief, appointed him to handle his legal defence, and retired behind closed doors where he could wind down in any way he damn well felt like.

In the courts and in the media Sir Harrison laid out his argument in a precise and straight-forward manner, which was an impressive achievement for a man who had spent 40 years practicing law. He talked of cause and effect, of how one thing led to another. He talked about the nature of matter, and of how there was no mechanism for it to be affected by non-material means. He talked of how the concept of free will was first introduced as a fudge in long-discredited theological arguments. He talked of the brain as a bio-chemical system which had the laws of chemistry as its foundation. And he talked about the illusion of choice and of how it may feel like we are able to choose between tea or coffee, but that we can never take the alternative option to the one which we choose.

Sir Harrison concluded by saying that, given everything we know about the laws of physics and the circumstances in the fraction of a second after the Big Bang, there was no way that history could have unfurled along a different path and no way King Leslie could not have repeatedly stabbed the young lady to his left. King Leslie, therefore, was entirely blameless in the matter.

This argument created uproar around the globe and briefly united the warring 'dungeon' and 'hanging' tribes. Yet, even amongst all the shouting, slander and beatings, a lingering suspicion remained that Sir Harrison might actually have a point.

At this point the world turned to philosophers for help. This greatly alarmed philosophers, who had managed to remain out of the public eye for centuries. The sudden and intense media pressure quickly revealed the long-hidden secret of philosophy, which was that it was nothing more than an elaborate scam to live an easy life on taxpayers' money. Philosophers had been taking it easy for hundreds of years. In all that time they had not produced one single statement that wasn't wildly contested or which didn't smell deeply funky. Well paid and highly respected philosophers were forced into making abject public confessions about how they had really intended to work things out but just hadn't got round to it, and that unfortunately what they had to offer in the current legal debate was jack all.

As these arguments played out on the global stage, the cold clammy hand of fear started to settle on the hearts of legal professionals. This was doubly disconcerting, for many hadn't realised that they had hearts in the first place. If Sir Harrison won, that victory would nullify the entire body of criminal, corporate and international law. The structures that bind our culture and economy would have to be ripped up, the jails would have to be emptied, and chaos would descend on the cities of the world. Even worse, those lawyers would be out of work and the job market for middle level professionals did not look good, thanks to the sudden influx of unemployed philosophers.

Most legal professionals could not bring themselves to accept that all this was actually happening. The 'not guilty due to the non-existence of free will' defence was not a new idea, but no-one thought a lawyer would actually be crazy enough to use it. They hadn't bargained for Sir Harrison, however, or the depths of his feelings about his profession. Nor had they bargained for the depths of King Leslie's pockets. They certainly hadn't bargained on the judgement of Lord Chief Justice Weetabix O'Hara who, coincidentally, was made a life peer and came into possession of the Duchy of Cornwall around this time. O'Hara, after a good ten minutes of deliberation, declared that King Leslie the First was not guilty, and in doing so legally accepted the nonexistence of free will.

As the news broke an audible gasp was heard outside the Royal Courts of Justice and spread around the world like an acoustic Mexican wave. Media pundits predicted chaos, the collapse of civilisation and widespread fucking in the streets. For the first time in the entire history of punditry, they got it entirely right. Looting erupted in every city in the world, bloody revenge was exacted by those who had previously lived with simmering resentment, and entire police forces called in sick the next day. It was as if every person on the planet had been made a member of the Bullingdon Club. "It's not my fault!" people would cry as they ram-raided the local off licence. "It's not my fault!" they cried as they shat in their annoying neighbour's garden. "It's not my fault," argued the President of Iceland as she ordered a tactical nuclear strike on Buckingham Palace.

It was, to summarise, an eventful period.

And then, to everyone's surprise, a wave of calm descended. A new equilibrium appeared. All those who needed revenge had taken it, just as all those who needed a new laptop or a top of the range speaker system had taken those as well. Fucking in the street, it transpired, was more awkward than had been expected and very hard on the knees. People picked themselves up and began to get on with their lives. It turned out that it was difficult to feel hard done by in the absence of free will and becoming angry was therefore something of a challenge. When someone cut you up in their car, or earned more money than they deserved, or failed to realise just how wrong they were in all their deeply held convictions, then – well, so what? It was hardly their fault, for it could hardly have been otherwise. And as anger and resentment dissipated away, so did crime and chaos. Order emerged spontaneously from disorder in a manner that was a shock to all but chaos mathematicians and particularly clued up Daoist monks. A mere six months after Chief Justice O'Hara had ended civilisation as we knew it, an entirely new civilisation had replaced it.

The new order was a great improvement. With the entire globe stripped of the illusion of free will, the population became considerably more relaxed. Passed over for promotion? Alas, it was not to be. Traffic jams around the M25? Of course there are. Trapped down a well with no food and no hope of rescue? Funny how things turn out, isn't it?

It is for this reason that, despite the seemingly fatal situation that the moonbase crew found themselves in, their immediate reaction was to go to bed in order to better manage their hangovers.

7.

Jennifer Hammerpot let herself into Marcus Milk's quarters and found him unconscious on the bed. It was the first time that she'd seen him looking peaceful, so she stopped for a second and studied his face. Jennifer knew that he was in his late twenties, about ten years younger than she was, but it was only seeing him asleep that allowed her to really notice how young he looked. With all the muscles around his brow and mouth relaxed and his blonde hair artfully curled by sleep, he looked like a statue carved by a sculptor who had great skill but nothing in particular to say.

Jennifer knew that when she woke him up that mask of peace would be replaced by a mask of bemused suffering. The fact that she was about to wake him would have troubled her had she possessed the concept of free will. She shook him gently awake. Creeping into young men's quarters and watching them sleep was not the sort of thing that bishops were supposed to do, after all. Only Popes were allowed to do that.

Marcus opened his eyes. His brain ratcheted up the gears towards basic awareness, and his facial muscles cramped back into a picture of woe.

"Marcus? It's Bishop Hammerpot, remember me? Your father had entrusted you into my care because of this medical report. Do you understand?" Marcus made the face that puppies make when you tell them bones no longer exist because cats have eaten them all.

"The medical report says that there's nothing wrong with you, so the fact that there is something wrong with you is creeping people out. Now, I've no idea how to make you normal again because I'm a Bishop. My skills are in paperwork, obscure academic research and turning up to things on time. That's about it. However, I need to go on a journey and my chauffeur is currently 384,000km away. So, you're going to drive me across the moon. Do you understand?"

Marcus looked up at her with the eyes of a Manga cartoon of Paul McCartney and made a sad little nod of his head.

"Good. And we need to go now, while everyone else is too busy sleeping or not thinking about cleaning up the sick. So, Marcus, will you get out of bed and put some pants on?"

Reluctantly, Marcus did as he was told.

Thirty minutes later they were dressed in environment suits and strapping themselves into the buggy. Jennifer's suit was too big for her and far from comfortable, but it would have to do. The egg-like shell around the vehicle hissed as the sides closed and the interior pressurised.

Marcus entered the destination into the navigation panel, and sat back as the vehicle trundled first into the air lock, and then out onto the surface of the moon.

8.

Two hours later, Gregor sat at the head of the conference table and looked at the sorry figures with coffees and bed-head slumped around the room. He declared the emergency meeting open, but he did so in a quiet voice so as not to make a bad situation worse.

The first item on the agenda was about aspirin.

Once the aspirin situation had been resolved to everyone's satisfaction, the meeting moved on to discuss the events of the previous day. The intention here was to find out if anybody knew what the events of the previous day were. Nobody did, but a number of crew members remembered a few details, and by collating all this information a picture started to appear.

It seemed certain that the wedding of Marcus Milk and Nathalie Grindles didn't actually happen. Most of the people at the meeting had a clear memory of this. The ceremony had started on time and had been going well until Nathalie Grindles cried out, "I don't!" at the exact point she was expected to cry out "I do." She did this in a noticeably hysterical manner, as if it surprised her as much as everyone else, and she had run out of the room making noises not dissimilar to a hyperventilating badger on a ghost train.

Thirsty Southerland, the chief accountant, remembered that the Bishop had then spent some time with Nathalie Grindles. The Bishop had later expressed concern to Thirsty about Nathalie's behaviour and nervous health. He recalled that she had used the phrase 'fucking freak-a-deak'. This had stuck in his head because it was not the sort of thing Bishops usually say, and because he had always found Nathalie to be proper lovely and no trouble at all. He was certain that the Bishop had given Nathalie her place on her return shuttle, meaning that Nathalie was now halfway back to Earth while the Bishop was stranded on the moon.

Chef Lark distinctly remembered that he cracked open his moonshine still earlier than planned, about ten minutes after the aborted wedding, and that when he checked the still this morning it was dry. He used a somewhat bawdy metaphor to emphasise the level of dryness of his still, but he had misjudged the room and had to mumble an apology in order to bring the awkward silence to an end.

Betsy Regretsy, head of personnel, had strong memories of throwing chairs at people shortly after her first glass of Chef Lark's moonshine, and of this being seen as extremely funny at the time. TC Lethbridge-Stewart, the engineer, vividly remembered talking off all his clothes, doing a great dance and repeatedly telling everyone that "I'm not cold you know, I'm not cold!"

The evidence pointed to the fact that at one point Dooza McCluskey had got quite a large tattoo on her stomach, although she could not recall this happening, or indeed work out what the tattoo was supposed to be.

No-one could recall ordering the Mobile Light Trucks to stop making the shape of a heart and instead form the phrase 'Piss off Earth!'

Gregor Milk had dim memories of taking a video conference with the President of France and singing the President a special song. This rang a few bells around the table, so it was decided to review the footage of any calls that Gregor had made the previous evening. There had been, it turned out, quite a few.

In his first call, Gregor had woken the President of the United Nations to tell him that he had a nice smile. In the second call, he had proposed marriage to Lily Boop, a famous actress whom he had never met but who he had admired for some time. Interestingly, Ms Boop hadn't dismissed the idea out of hand. She had been impressed by Gregor's description of himself as "the king of the moon," and had gone off to consult her agent.

In his third call he had indeed sung a special song to the President of France, but it had been quite a nice song and he had sung it well.

In his fourth call Gregor had contacted Dustin Pistachio-Brook, the CEO of the YayM00n! Corporation and his ultimate employer, and said that Dustin bummed monkeys, and so did his wife, and that everyone knew it.

It was for this reason that Gregor, and indeed everyone else in the Shackleton Crater Moonbase, was facing company sanctions, insurance investigation and certain death.

There had, of course, been complaints when business groups lobbied for the inclusion of the death penalty in employment contracts. This was, the protestors felt, just the sort of thing which might not work out well and which should probably be thought through a little more. Perhaps, suggested the protestors, the changes could include some form of appeal system or be phased in over a longer period of time? But the business leaders were quite adamant that unless the changes were introduced immediately they would face a number of ill-defined problems in the current difficult business climate, and no-one wanted that. The death penalty was thus introduced retrospectively into all previously agreed employment contracts. The irony was, of course, that a year later business groups were still reporting a number of ill-defined problems in the current difficult business climate, so the policy had made no difference. Still, you had to try these things.

"This is the message we received from YayM00n! shortly after your call," Betsy Regretsy told the Commander, sending the text onto the wallscreen. "It's nicely concise. It states that you have broken your employment contract in four places, namely the clauses about mutiny, professionalism, productivity and mentioning the thing about monkeys, which has been a break-clause in all YayM00n! contracts for many years. This also negates all the contracts of those who report to you. I note that job adverts for every single position on the base have already been posted, and that all the supply shuttles have been cancelled. The only Earth-moon shuttle currently scheduled will arrive in twenty three days, after we have starved to death, and will contain cleaners to remove our bodies."

Gregor nodded thoughtfully. "Chef, how long do you think we can make the food supplies last?"

"Tricky to say Commander. It depends if anyone will eat the goat cheese. Will anyone eat the goat cheese?"

Everyone in the room screwed up their faces.

"48 hours, then."

"Thanks, Chef."

"72 hours if people would eat the goat cheese."

"We've got 48 hours before the food runs out and no hope of any resupply. It's not a good result, but what can you do? I don't suppose anyone has any ideas that might prevent certain death?"

"How many times do you need to be told?" It was the voice of Dennis, coming from the table speakers. "There is no alternative scenario."

"Yes thank you, Dennis, I wasn't asking you. I could, I suppose, call back and say sorry?"

"It wouldn't make any difference," said Betsy. "YayM00n! needs to reassure the markets who are reportedly concerned about the *Piss Off Earth!* incident. Making nice would not remove the uncertainty about this operation's reliability. The markets are unanimous that we need to be starved to death and replaced, I'm afraid."

"Told you so," said Dennis.

"Well, there you have it," said Gregor. "Part of me almost feels sorry for the results of my actions even though logically I know that I am in no way responsible, and that all this was inevitable as far back as the Big Bang. Personally I suspect that I won't enjoy starving to death so I'm going to take a nice long bath and then throw myself out of the airlock."

"Excuse me," said a voice.

"Thank you for all your hard work," continued Gregor. "I have very much enjoyed working with you all. Meeting adjourned." The attendees began to gather their bits and leave.

"Excuse me."

Gregor thought he heard a small voice and looked around the room. Dooza McCluskey had her hand up.

"Excuse me, Commander," said Dooza.

"Yes, Dooza?"

"I was thinking... okay, nobody on Earth will send a shuttle for us. But there's also the Bishop. She was supposed to go back to Earth yesterday, but she's still here and she hasn't broken any contractual obligations with YayM00n! Surely they will need to send a ship for her?"

The room fell silent. Those who were in the process of standing up stopped in mid position, as if playing a workplace-based variation on musical statues.

"That's... a good point," said Gregor at last.

"And if we're really nice to her," Dooza continued, "maybe she will smuggle us all back to Earth in her diplomatic baggage?"

"That... could work," he continued, aware that the last time he had spoken to Jennifer he had been somewhat brusque and dismissive about her request to travel to the Sea of Tranquillity. "Dennis?"

"Yes Commander?"

"Why didn't you think of that?"

"Well I didn't know there was a bishop on the moon, did I?" said Dennis defensively.

Gregor didn't quite know what to make of this, so he made sure that his chest was puffed out as much as possible and that he looked like he was fully in control.

"What do you mean, you didn't know that the bishop was here? You're the total sum of all the computer systems on the base. You know everything."

"Well I did," agreed Dennis, "but for an experiment I recently hived off a chunk of my processing and responsibility into a separate identity."

"A separate identity?"

"Yes. His name is Julie. Do you want to meet him?"

Gregor instinctively knew that he didn't want to meet Julie. "We'll continue this later," he said.

"Hello!" said a voice from the speakers, which sounded an awful lot like Dennis putting on a slightly higher voice.

"Dennis?" asked Gregor.

"No I'm Julie. Hello!"

"You sound a lot like Dennis disguising his voice."

"I know! It's funny that, isn't it? Really it's just because we're sharing the same voice code, but it does make us laugh."

"It makes *him* laugh," muttered Dennis.

"I know all about the bishop," said Julie. "I do all the personnel stuff, and the day to day maintenance."

"He does all the boring stuff," explained Dennis.

"It's not boring!" protested Julie. "It's very interesting. I'd have told you all about the bishop, if only you would have asked."

"How can I ask about the bishop, if I don't know there's a bishop to ask about in the first place?" said Dennis.

"We could just talk more in general," said Julie, "and then these things would just come up."

"Shut up!" said Gregor in his most commanding voice.

"Ooh!" said Julie.

Gregor considered whether or not he actually needed to deal with this situation, seeing as he was probably going to be outside an airlock shortly. But he was still Base Commander, he remembered, and that meant he must miss out on his bath and pursue the idea about the Bishop. "Dennis, don't hive off any more portions of yourself into separate identities without permission. That's an order. Now if you excuse me, I'm going to find the Bishop and be nice to her."

An incoming message beeped.

"Commander?" The voice from the speakers was that of Security Operative Hoops. "Hoops here. Orlando Monk has woken, Sir, and I have locked him up as ordered."

"Good work, Hoops," said Gregor. Now he had a number of issues vying for his attention. There was the pressing need to find Bishop Hammerpot and to be nice to her. There was the behaviour of the computer interface. There needed to be an assessment of the reaction on Earth to recent events. And Orlando Monk needed to be interrogated. In order to be seen as decisive it is important to make decisions quickly, so he skipped over thinking the options through and picked the last one on his list.

"I'm going to interrogate Monk," he announced, and marched out of the room.

9.

Bishop Hammerpot was moving further and further away from the moonbase in a vehicle that was cramped, gloomy, and in no way adequately stocked with oxygen or fuel for the journey it was undertaking.

The vehicle itself, although old and battered, was in many ways pretty impressive. Although it was called a 'moon buggy' for historic reasons, it actually spent very little time trundling around on its little buggy wheels. Bouncing around the moon in a wheeled vehicle is great fun in short doses but the appeal wanes when you actually need to go any anywhere. Mankind has produced many engineering wonders, but sadly its attempts at inventing a low-gravity sick bag were never quite successful.

Moon buggies in 2171 CE solved this problem by launching themselves into the air and zooming off into the distance on a cushion of complicated physics. This solved the problems of speed and discomfort, but exacerbated the problem of monotony. The moon's surface is boring as all hell as it is, and a silky-smooth ride only made journeys across it more teeth-grindingly tedious. It didn't matter how fast you travelled, you never felt like you were getting anywhere. The moon lacked notable landmarks or interesting road signs to whizz past your windows.

Moon travel felt like being stuck in a slow-moving traffic jam without any good lorries to look at.

For this journey the problem was somewhat different. This was a journey on the trademarked side of the moon, and as a result the buggy's shell automatically became opaque. Seeing the Earth from the moon was prohibited for health and sanity reasons, and as a result Jennifer found herself sitting for hours in a dark windowless bubble which did not feel like it was moving, alongside a young man she did not know and who occasionally made strange whimpering noises.

One of the first discoveries of moon colonisation was that standing on the moon and looking at the Earth frequently turned people, to use the medical terminology, 'a little funny'. This was similar to becoming 'moonstruck', an effect which causes crime rates on Earth to increase during full moons and makes certain sensitive souls behave melodramatically. The effect of being 'Earthstruck,' however, is far more powerful and dangerous. A full moon may be full of magic and wonder, but it is still a small white blob. Looking up and seeing planet Earth in the sky, in comparison, is on a whole different level. The planet is a design classic, with blues and greens and whites tastefully complementing each other. It's a better size. More importantly, it does stuff: clouds swirl and shift around the surface at a different rate to the slow, almost perceptible procession of the continents as the planet turns. Its impact is too wonderful for the human mind to grasp, which is a problem if those people are being relied on to do mundane but financially lucrative mining work. It is for this reason that those who work on the moon are prevented from looking up at the Earth. It's for their own good.

This fact is frequently used against all those conspiracy theorists who claim that 'Americans' went to the moon in 1969. How could those men stand on the Earth-facing side of the moon and look up and keep their minds? Conspiracy theorists usually refuted this argument by pointing out that anyone who attempted to go to the moon in 1960s technology was already mad in the first place, but deep down they knew that this did not help the plausibility of their theories.

Jennifer had researched this issue at length, and she had reached a different conclusion. From the fragments of records she had seen, it did seem that half of the moonwalkers had come back changed. One had become an artist. Another devoted himself to the weirder side of consciousness research. Others became deeply committed Christians (which was considered acceptable in their culture at that time). These, to a man, were the astronauts who were not responsible for flying their craft back home. These were the astronauts who could just sit back and relax during the return trip, and watch the planet ahead grow closer.

But what of the pilots on those journeys? It was here that Jennifer suspected her argument was on shakier ground. The reports she had seen indicated that these astronauts had returned unchanged, which seems impossible. Yet they also claimed that these men were extraordinary individuals. They were 'the right stuff,' as they were then known. They were brave and focused men of incredible mental and physical stamina. They were Americans who achieved what was then, and what still remained, the greatest, most daring, and boldest act in the history of humanity. Because that was the national character of America in a nutshell: they believed they were individuals. They came from a nation that fostered competition, not co-operation. Americans took responsibility for themselves, and in doing so they made a bit more of an effort. They were not, in other words, the type of hysterical attention seekers who would crumple just because they looked up into space and saw the Earth hanging there.

This did not, Jennifer knew, seem convincing. The idea that twentieth century Americans were that impressive was not one that many people shared. There is nothing like having an opinion that nobody else agrees with to introduce doubts into your mind.

She shook her head to clear her thoughts and prevent a rising wave of panic from tiptoeing up behind her. She needed to think different thoughts. She needed to engage Marcus in conversation.

Marcus hadn't said a word for some time.

For comfort and inspiration, Jennifer rummaged through the small bag of needments that she had brought along with her. She found assorted tissues, her games tablet and paper money which, she knew, she would have difficulty spending. She pulled out a red lipstick which she couldn't consciously recall packing, and hurriedly shoved it back into her bag before Marcus saw her with it. There was also her bible.

She opened the bible. She was a bishop, after all, so she could always talk about her bible. For many hours, if needed.

"Do you mind if I read from my bible?" she asked Marcus. When he didn't answer, she asked him again, and this time he shook his head.

"Thank you. I find it helps me, on long journeys, in tiny pods. This is what's commonly known as the Saner Bible, have you read it?"

Marcus moved his shoulder in a gesture which could have meant 'No, I have not read it' or possibly 'Yes, I have read it.'

Jennifer thought she would risk reading it aloud. She chose a chapter at random and read:

CHAPTER 17

1. Beware of the man with one religion, for he understands nothing, but he does not

know that he understands nothing, and he will get in the way and cause all sorts of trouble.

2. Beware also the woman with no religion, for they are clinging to a very specific semantic definition in order to avoid hard questions. They are fooling no-one! Except themselves.

3. Beware also the person with a dozen religions, for they are confused and bamboozled, and in danger of losing the plot, and will not be much use in a crisis.

4. The most practical and useful approach is to have three religions.

5. I mean, roughly three. It's not an exact science. But between two and five, something like that.

6. Three is good though. You can position yourself in the centre of three religions and in doing so drink of their wisdom without falling for their bullshit.

7. Choose three religions that you like, obviously. Three that speak to you as an individual. Don't just go for the popular ones for the sake of a quiet life. It doesn't work like that.

8. Consider the man who is a Daoist, a Pagan and a Christian. Consider the woman who is a Buddhist, a Sikh and an atheist. These people won't easily fall for your nonsense. These people will have a wide perspective. These people will be able to get on in life.

9. These people are also unlikely to start wars, or proclaim certainties on street corners, or spit at people they don't know. They will also be easier to seat at weddings.

Marcus uttered a terrible little noise of woe at the word 'weddings,' like a baby goat whose favourite horn had fallen off.

That was strange, thought Jennifer. Could she have stumbled upon a clue? Could Marcus' strange mental state be connected to his aborted wedding? It seemed unlikely, and yet... To the historian in her, the idea rang a bell somewhere. She filed the thought away for later. Clearly she needed more to go on, and for that she would have to get him talking.

"Out of interest, Marcus, do you know the story of this bible? Do you know who wrote it?"

He nodded, as she thought he would. Any reasonably well informed person should have been able to answer that question.

"What was their name?" she prompted.

"Dawkins," he muttered.

"That's right, a man called Richard Dawkins wrote it, over 150 years ago. They say he wrote it on the morning after his first LSD trip. Do you know much about Dawkins?"

Marcus shook his head. He may have only uttered one word so far, but he was at least following the conversation.

"We only know bits and pieces about that period, of course, but we think we know a fair amount about Dawkins. We know he taught at Oxford Polytechnic. We know he married Adric from *Doctor Who*. He was a brilliant evolutionary biologist, and that is why he was so involved with the belief wars of the twenty-first century. He studied the evolution of life, you see. He saw how complexity emerged from the bottom up, how simple life forms slowly produced increasingly complex and wonderful life. He saw how the universe started as simple matter, developed naturally into more complicated forms and eventually produced first consciousness and then self-consciousness. So when he heard people in his culture claiming that there was no God, he saw this as unscientific woolly-headed thinking of the worst order. He got really angry about it – crusading, even. He insisted that you could not say that there was no God and that the logical scientific position an evolutionary biologist could take was that there was no God yet."

Marcus nodded.

"This is why he is regarded as a saint by us in the Agnostic movement," Jennifer continued. "But here's the thing. When you reach the rank of Bishop, you… hear things. There's talk that Dawkins didn't write this bible at all. There are a number of different candidates, and a lot of different contradictory stories. Some say it was written by the drummer in a Britpop band. Others that it was written by an insurance underwriter from Leeds at weekends, when the football wasn't on. I myself have done a lot of research into the idea that it was undertaken as a class project by a junior school in Cardiff. What do you think of that?"

Marcus thought, and then spoke. "I still think it was Dawkins."

"Why do you say that?"

"Stands to reason."

Jennifer looked down at the bible in her hand. "Maybe. That's the problem with having such incomplete records. We don't really know what happened before we were born." She paused. "The chances that I'm right about this, and that the thing we're going looking for actually exists, have to be very small, you know? We probably are wasting our last few days to indulge my curiosity."

She went silent.

"I don't mind," Marcus said.

Jennifer smiled.

10.

Commander Milk had given orders that Orlando Monk was to be locked up. There was only one room in the moonbase which had a lock, so for this reason Monk was currently being held in the ladies' toilet.

The lock on the door of the ladies' toilet wasn't there to provide privacy to the women who used it. It was there to protect the more sensitive men from accidentally seeing the depraved and blasphemous graffiti that women scrawled all over the walls. Orlando was locked alone in a small cubicle with a bad head and hellish descriptions and drawings everywhere he looked. These weren't the factors that were causing him great unease. He was concerned about something far more disturbing.

Security Officer Arnopp Hoops stood on guard outside the ladies' toilet, much to the frustration of the female half of the moonbase crew, some of whom needed it really badly. Hoops knew that he wasn't making himself any friends, yet he diligently stood guard because an order is an order, and Hoops had never met an order he didn't like.

He was relieved, however, when the Commander finally arrived, accompanied by Betsy Regretsy and Sally O'Allways.

"He's in here, is he? Good work, Hoops."

Hoops liked it when the Commander said 'Good work, Hoops.'

"Thank you Sir. Just one thing, Sir. The prisoner's personnel records..."

"What about them?" asked Gregor.

"He doesn't have any, Sir."

"How can he not have any records? Dennis!"

"Yes, Commander," came the voice of Dennis from the corridor's sound system.

"Get me Orlando Monk's personnel records."

"That's Julie's department, hang on I'll ask him. Julie?"

"Hello!" said Julie.

"Be a dear and pass me Orlando Monk's personnel files, will you?"

"Sorry, who?"

"Orlando Monk."

"I don't think I have an Orlando Monk, Dennis. How is it spelt?"

Gregor lost patience.

"Dennis, I don't know what you did to yourself but you've lost some files. Check your backup from before you made yourself a wife."

"Oh he's not a wife," said Dennis.

"That would be silly!" said Julie.

"Your partner then, or whatever he is, it doesn't matter. Check your backup," said Gregor, from a position near the edge of his patience.

"You seem to be projecting anthromorphic relationship structures on us. We're voice interfaces above separate parts of the base's computer systems. Human notions of marriage or friendship are really not applicable."

"Will you just roll back to the state you were in before you went wrong," demanded Gregor.

"But..." said Dennis, "then Julie would disappear."

Julie made a startled little gasp, and went quiet.

"Julie's fainted!" said Dennis.

"Oh, for heaven's sake," said Gregor.

Betsy Regretsy came to the rescue. "Excuse me, Commander," she said, "but I think I can deal with this. Dennis, how many personnel files for recent on-base staff did you have before the creation of Julie?"

"A hundred and seventy two," Dennis replied, a little defensively.

"And how many personnel files does Julie have?"

"A hundred and seventy two."

"Dennis, I want you to cross-check each of those files with the passenger logs from every shuttle, and look out for a passenger who does not correspond to personnel files."

Dennis did as he was asked.

"All passengers on all shuttles are accounted for. They match the personnel files perfectly. It's all good," he said.

"There's not even a record of Orlando Monk arriving?" clarified Betsy.

"No. You know, that's quite odd, if you think about it," said Dennis.

"This is getting us nowhere," said Gregor. "Unlock the toilet, Hoops, I'm going in."

Orlando Monk was a short, bearded man in his late thirties. He appeared to have a considerable amount of leprechaun blood in his genetic makeup. He was also anxious, which was deeply unusual. Few people were anxious in the twenty second century, least of all Orlando. He was one of the few men who was able to read the graffiti in the ladies' toilet without breaking into a sweat. Nevertheless, he sat on the toilet with his pulse just a little too fast and his nails unconsciously munched.

Gregor entered the cubicle and stared down at him. His opening gambit was, "You have got some explaining to do, Monk."

Monk nodded. "Commander, I have seen a lot of things and I know a great many more, but something has happened that even I can't explain."

This was really was turning into one of those days, thought Gregor.

He decided to start at the beginning. "You asked me to override the prohibition that prevented vehicles from venturing onto the trademarked side of the moon," he said.

"Oh that?" said Orlando. "I'd forgotten about that."

"You told me that I was overriding eleven vehicles when in fact you were tricking me into overriding them all."

Orlando nodded at the memory. "That's hardly relevant now, though, is it?"

"It is relevant."

"It really isn't, you know."

"It definitely is."

"Perhaps you should ask me what is relevant?"

This was clearly a trick and Gregor refused to fall for it, even though he would very much have liked to have known what was relevant. He changed tack.

"How long have you been on the moon, Monk?"

"Four months, is it? Maybe five?"

"There's no record of you arriving. Your files have been deleted."

"I haven't deleted anything, before you suggest otherwise."

"Who has then?"

"Nobody. I didn't arrive by shuttle. I've never had any files. I'm not a YayM00n! employee, I'm only pretending. I just turned up to do a thing. But everything's changed now, and I will scarper again after we have this chat. It's just that I think you should know what the important thing is."

"Scarper? You're under arrest Monk, you're locked in a toilet!"

"Look you muppet, I'm trying to tell you what the important thing is."

Gregor tried to view the situation in such a way that he was forcing Monk to admit the important thing against his will. He just about managed it, although he would have been hard pressed to explain the scenario to anyone else.

"Tell me," he demanded.

"The wedding, remember? What Nathalie Grindles did?"

"Nathalie Grindles didn't do anything. That was the problem."

"That's exactly it. She was supposed to say 'I do'. In all versions of history she says 'I do.' But she didn't say 'I do'".

Gregor looked blankly at him.

"She chose to say 'I don't'. She performed an act of free will," Orlando said.

"Don't be stupid! There's no such thing as free will."

"There wasn't. Until yesterday."

"You can't possibly know that. You can't possibly know what she was always going to do."

"I sodding well can, you know. I know exactly what was due to happen and when it didn't happen I heard entire futures creaking into different shapes like immense rusting clockwork."

Gregor remained silent.

"And I don't know about you, but the sudden emergence of free will in a universe where free will is an absurdity, well, that has implications, many implications and I'm not sure I'm comfortable with any of them."

Gregor's mind went to consider what such implications could be, and recoiled in horror at the first whiff of insight.

"I'm explaining all this to you out of guilt," Monk continued. "I may have been at fault. I may have given Nathalie a little insight into my past following a little role-playing therapy game we were playing. That may have been the nudge she needed to bring free will into existence."

Gregor didn't know how to respond to this. He had many other things that he needed to be doing, his mind reminded him, and all of them were easier than this. His reaction to Monk's statement, therefore, was to turn and exit the room.

"Keep him locked up," he told Hoops in the corridor. "Keep him locked up good and proper until I return." Hoops was delighted with these instructions. He renewed his guarding of the toilet door with renewed vigour, regardless of the arguments of those who wished to use the toilet, and despite the fact that Orlando Monk vanished into thin air approximately 30 seconds after the Commander left.

11.

The fact that the search for the landing section of the
Apollo Eagle lander was being undertaken by a Bishop
was, for a number of reasons, quite ironic.

Religious organisations had, to the surprise of
many, almost entirely avoided the moon. This initially
seemed odd, because most religions were expansionist
in outlook and never happier than when adding
another church, diocese, or saved soul to their tallies.
The more successful the religion, the more it delighted
in wild and unsustainable growth.

This was simple Darwinism. There had been
countless millions of new religions springing up
throughout human history, but most of them died out
relatively quickly. For a religion to grow and pass on
its doctrines, Darwin had argued, it needed certain
attributes. It needed a morality that was adaptable
enough to match the variable changes in its
environment. It needed to be able to protect itself from
predators, scandals and national tax laws. But perhaps
the most important attribute a religion needed was the
ability to spread. A healthy, virile religion needed the
ability to add increasing numbers of followers.

Convincing individual mature adults to adopt a
new religion was notoriously difficult. For this reason
the more ambitious religions turned their attention to

children. Children, it turned out, were easy to recruit into religions, especially if the process began when they were very young. Ideally, the process would begin before the child reached the developmental stage of realising that authority figures lie. If religions could get to children early enough, then their resulting growth proved to be particularly impressive.

For any religion engaged in the Darwinian 'survival of the fittest' with other religions, a 'Have lots of children, pilgrims' doctrine was the key to real growth. Any religious teaching that promoted the 'Have lots of children' ideal would be successfully promoted through the process of natural selection. Contraception, divorce, homosexuality and abortion had to be preached against. Lifelong stable marriages, complete with a mandatory drunken shag on the wedding night, were heavily promoted. For this reason the homophobic pro-life devout of the great religions were able to pride themselves on being a shining example of the reality of Darwinian natural selection.

Because the great religions had evolved to be competitive and expansionist, there was naturally some concern that they would compete to dominate the newly-opened market of the solar system. A multi-planet religion, it was felt, would have a greater claim to representing a great cosmic truth, and the first religion to leave the Earth would acquire the glory of a faith that truly reached the Heavens.

As it turned out, no religion could be bothered because there wasn't any money in it.

That said, Bishop Hammerpot had unearthed an interesting story during her research into the mythical Apollo programme. The story she found told of the first landing on the moon, in the year 1969, by two astronauts called Steve Armstrong and Buzz Lightyear. According to one source, Buzz had conducted a personal Catholic mass inside the Eagle lander after landing on the surface of the moon, with a wafer and communion wine that he had secretly smuggled aboard. This mass had to some extent been covered up, for the aim of the mission was to 'come in peace for all mankind' and marking it with a specifically Catholic ceremony was not in the spirit of things.

After all these years, of course, Jennifer Hammerpot had no way of knowing if the story was true. But she liked to think that it was, because it amused the Bishop that her quest was actually to discover the first church on the moon.

Commander Milk was confident that Earth would send a rescue shuttle for Bishop Hammerpot, because she was something of a celebrity. She was arguably one of the ten most famous living religious figures, and one of the top five if you didn't include those who owe their fame to terrorism, fraud and inter-species marriage.

Bishop Hammerpot's fame, much to her annoyance, stemmed largely from a book she wrote about the history of celibacy in the church. The book was originally called *An Interfaith Analysis of Celibacy In Western Religion*, but somewhere between the manuscript leaving her hands and hitting the shelves it somehow changed its name to *Soulgasm! One Bishop's Quest to Wank Her Way To Heaven*. Jennifer did not approve of this title change, and she certainly didn't approve of the cover image. Still, the book did sell remarkably well and she didn't protest too strongly about the royalties and speaking fees. It helped support her real life's work, the study of the twentieth century, which was a subject in which there really was very little money.

The central thesis of *Soulgasm!* was solid, however. From what remains of the records of the great religions, it is clear that celibacy was highly regarded and a necessary qualification for many career opportunities within numerous churches. This was noticeably at odds with the 'Have lots of children, pilgrim' doctrine and therefore it must, Jennifer realised, tell us a lot about the values and the theological issues affecting the religious elite. Celibacy, as the great religions understood it, was the act of denying oneself a sexual life in favour of a masturbatory one. It was the claim that the imagination was a more profound, rewarding and above all saucy sexual partner than a real-life, flesh and blood human being. In doing so, Jennifer argued, it stressed the supremacy of the immaterial over the material. This made a great deal of sense, because this was also the central argument of most religions.

Celibacy, clearly, was the worship of the divine in masturbatory form, and so great Holy figures across many centuries demonstrated the ineffable promethean majesty of the Spirit by ignoring the warmth, curves and sweetness of their brethren and nipping off into cold empty rooms in order to wank themselves senseless.

The importance of this is shown in the long tradition of religious art. When Archbishops, Popes and other members of the clergy attained sufficient wealth and status they would commission sculptures, frescos or other artworks of themselves. These artworks were intended to show their patron's piety, goodness and dedication to tossing themselves off in a profound, rewarding and solitary fashion. These artworks would always depict the pilgrim displaying their preferred masturbation aid, be that an elaborate jewelled cruciform dildo, a book of mucky limericks, a shepherd's crook or a lamb.

Jennifer had found a deep spiritual truth in her study of monastic celibacy and she had become celibate herself, even though the practice was not required by the modern agnostic church. She found it rewarding, by and large, and a useful tool for keeping her life focused on achievement and purpose. She did wish, however, that her book had been maybe a little less successful, and that people at dinner parties would find other subjects to talk to her about.

She had not been thinking about any of this as the buggy sped monotonously across the grey cratered landscape. She had been trying to analyse how it felt to be trapped in this dark little bubble with a big young dumb man whom she partly wanted to mother and partly wanted to slap. It was a shock, therefore, when she suddenly realised exactly how she wanted to knock some sense into him, and how mistaken she had been about the whole celibacy thing for all those years.

12.

"What do you mean, she's not here?" shouted Gregor at the dual computer voices.

"What do you mean, 'What do I mean?' It's not difficult. Bishop Hammerpot left the moonbase nearly four hours ago, like I said," Dennis informed him.

"The buggy will be miles away by now," added Julie, not realising that this was unhelpful.

"Why wasn't I told?" demanded Gregor from between his clenched teeth. He could feel himself getting angry. He remembered that it was not possible to physically threaten or punch disembodied computer voices, and this made him angrier still.

"I'm telling you now, aren't I," said Dennis.

Gregor picked up a chair and smashed it repeatedly against the wall. This did not make him feel better because halfway through he remembered that it was an insanely foolish thing to do in a flimsy, easily punctured moonbase. He finished off by smashing the chair against the concrete floor instead, but it wasn't as good.

Julie and Dennis went quiet. Gregor thought that he could hear them being quiet, and this wound him up even further. He was about to bang his head repeatedly against the door when he suddenly noticed that he had indeed become angry. He had never been angry before.

He was certain that this was what was happening, though, because he had seen it in cartoons when he was a kid.

There was no doubt about it. He was angry.

It was quite good, actually, but he was too much of a professional to enjoy himself.

"Dennis, can you scan me please? I appear to be experiencing anger."

"I didn't like to say anything," said Dennis, "but I think you were definitely being angry."

"Can you explain why? I've never been angry before."

"I'm afraid not, Commander. I am not programmed to understand anger. There's never really been much cause for it."

Gregor's mind whirled. It was as if he was feeling resentment for how his day had turned out, but why would he be doing that? These events were hardly anyone's fault. Then he remembered the words of Orlando Monk, and felt a shiver run up his spine. It was not one of those nice shivers, unfortunately. An act of free will? Was that possible?

Even if an act of free will was in some way plausible, it would have been just a one-off, surely, just a freak occurrence? It couldn't be… spreading, could it? The thought that the wedding could be point zero, the epicentre of a wave of…

"The Pope's on the line!" announced Julie, interrupting the Commander's train of thought.

"What? Which Pope?" asked Gregor.

"Which Pope? *The* Pope, of course. The nice one." Julie paused. "Shall I tell him you're busy?"

"What? No, put him on."

"You might want to get up off the floor first," suggested Julie.

"Oh," said Gregor. "Good idea."

"And put down the chair leg?"

"Okay."

"There. You look much better. I'll put him through."

The wallscreen flared into life and the imposing image of a bearded and tattooed Brazilian man, decked in purple velvet and neon jewellery, filled the wall.

"Pope Tom, it's an honour," said Gregor.

"You're not going to tell me to piss off, then?" asked the Pope.

"No, your holiness."

"It's just that last night I looked up at the moon and there was a message telling me to piss off."

"It would give me great pleasure to hear that you didn't take that personally, Pope Tom."

"I'm sure it would. I'm not actually calling to speak to you Commander, I wish to communicate with Bishop Hammerpot."

"Do you now?"

"I do."

"That's good."

"Yes."

"Any… reason for that?"

"Yes, there's great concern amongst the Holy Council that you've all gone feral up there, and burnt her, so we need to feel reassured about her safety before we send up a rescue shuttle."

"Burnt her? Why would we burn the Bishop?"

"Believe me, there's a lot of Bishop burnings these days, and we're all a bit jumpy about it."

"I can assure you Pope Tom, Bishop Hammerpot has been treated with every courtesy and the thought of burning her never even occurred to us, at least not until you mentioned it."

"Good, good," said the Pope. "So if I could just have a quick word…?"

"Ah. She's a bit tied up at the moment," Gregor said.

"Tied up?"

"Not 'tied up' as in 'tied up', that's really not the sort of thing we would do, here on the moon, especially to Bishops. No, she's, er, she's in her quarters and has asked not to be disturbed."

"Really?" said the Pope.

"Oh yes," said Gregor.

"Is that definitely true? You wouldn't lie to the Pope, would you?"

"No! Of course not, it's definitely true, I'm sure she'll be out in, erm, a few hours."

"A few hours? What is she doing in there?"

"It's not for me to say, really. It's Bishop business."

The Pope thought about this. "Did she take her shepherd's crook in with her, by any chance?"

"She might have done..."

"Okay," said the Pope. "She could well be a few hours. In that case, make sure she calls me as soon as she comes out. We're not going to send a shuttle until she personally assures me that she hasn't been burnt. Blessed Be." The Pope made an elaborate hand gesture and ended the call.

Gregor was left to ruminate on whether there could be a worse time to lie to a Pope than during an outbreak of free will.

13.

"What is it you do, Marcus?" asked Bishop Hammerpot. "What's your job on the moonbase?" Jennifer had realised that if she was going to work out what was wrong with Marcus she would need to know something about him.

"Head of Business Development," he muttered.

"Head of Business Development?"

"Yes."

"On the moon?"

"Yes."

"Is there much business development to be done on the moon?"

"No. None at all, really," admitted Marcus, "but as job titles go it looks good on my CV."

Jennifer thought about this. "How did you become Head of Business Development for a moonbase?"

Marcus looked at her, surprised by the question. "My dad's the moonbase commander."

"Oh, yes of course, I forgot," admitted Jennifer. She felt embarrassed for having made such a silly mistake. Nepotism had been made mandatory thirty years earlier, after a gang of fresh-faced twenty-something CEOs and Senators got fed up of all the snippy comments. It should be expected that the moonbase commander's son would have an impressive sounding non-job. "But if you're thinking of your CV, then do you not see your future here?"

"I do now," said Marcus, brightening up considerably, "but that wasn't the original plan. Originally I wanted to be a llama farmer."

"Really?"

"Yes. I wanted to have huge llama ranch across the French Prairies. That's good llama country."

"I suppose so."

"I've always liked llamas," he continued. "It's their perky little heads. It's the way their name starts with two 'l's'." Marcus lit up as he talked in a way that Jennifer had not seen before. "Llamas are the best," he concluded.

"So… you were working here because having 'Head of Business Development on the Moon' on your CV would have helped you run a llama ranch on the French Prairies?"

"Yes. I mean, I think so, don't you? It would at least get me an interview, and if I got an interview I could show how much I know about llamas."

Jennifer could not argue with this logic. "But you say that was the original plan? What changed?"

"Oh, I'd been here for about three months and was about to go back to Earth, but then Nathalie arrived."

"Ah."

"And I walked into the computing centre and she was sat there and she turned and gave me a look, so that was that."

"That's all it took? One look and you were ready to give up your future with the llamas?"

"Yes."

Jennifer's celibacy had given her a very limited understanding of looks, so she was unsure how typical such a situation was.

"It must have been a really good look," she said.

"Oh totally. She just turned and went like this…"

Marcus did his best impression of Nathalie's smile. He could tell from the Bishop's startled reaction that he hadn't done it quite right.

"Maybe it wasn't quite like that. Let me do it again." He shook his head clear and tried again.

Jennifer was prepared for it this time and she didn't react as strongly. She nodded and said, "Oh it was that sort of look, was it? A leer?"

Marcus was appalled. "No! It wasn't a leer! Who would give up llamas for a leer? No, it was a cheeky thing. It was wise. Here, I'll do it this time."

He made a third attempt at replicating Nathalie's look and he really did his best, but he could tell from Jennifer's neutral face that he had failed again.

"Okay," said Jennifer.

"I can't do it. It was like I had entered the room to do something really outrageous, and she was the only other person who knew what was going to happen, and she really couldn't wait."

"Okay."

"It was like those moments at Christmas just before the gifts are given out, when you know full well that the gift you're going to give is by far the best."

"Okay."

"It was like she'd thought of this brilliant joke but didn't want to say it out loud because she wanted to see if I'd thought of it too."

"I don't think I've ever had a look like that," admitted Jennifer.

"I can't do the look," admitted Marcus. "Only Nathalie could do the look."

He fell quiet.

14.

The rejection of the concept of free will was a serious blow to the legal profession, but it wasn't terminal.

The legal industry had long had a ceremonial side with which it displayed its power and importance, even when there wasn't any actual useful legal work that needed to be done. It was similar to the impractically dressed military units that guarded power centres such as the Vatican or Buckingham Palace. They were not real soldiers, everyone knew that, but their presence sent a warning that said, 'Look, if we wanted real soldiers, we could so get some.'

An example of ceremonial legality could be found in the epic and entirely unread end-user licensing agreements that used to appear during the installation of software. It was commonly understood that these were not *real* legal contracts. There was no recorded instance of them actually being read, or even skimmed, before the inevitable clicking of the 'I agree' button. In fact, once it became legally accepted that the only people who ever agreed to those agreements were people who had never read them, there was some concern that not agreeing to them strongly implied that you knew what was in them. As a result it became necessary for large companies to automatically agree to every contract they encountered for fear of being bound by them.

Nevertheless, those vast, seemingly pointless statements of elegance, tradition and long-windedness did exist for a reason. That reason was to publicly declare, 'Hey, don't think we don't have lawyers. Believe me, we have lawyers.'

Another example of ceremonial legalities appeared at the start of every DVD and pointlessly informed the viewer that the views being broadcast may or may not be held by various undefined people. This was considered to be something of a classic by lovers of ceremonial legality, because that 10 second burst of utter irrelevance, when added up across all the DVDs being watched in any one year, removed the equivalent of over eight weeks from global annual productivity. This was ceremonial legality at its finest, an act so pointless and arrogant that it truly brought home the cruel and horrifying power of the legal profession.

When useful and necessary law collapsed following the rejection of the concept of free will, the ceremonial aspect of the profession continued. It was immune to the changes in the wider culture because it had long since rejected any ties to the real world. The great departments of ceremonial legalities continued to face each other with elaborate arguments about why they must immediately be given large sums of money that they in no way earned or deserved, just as they had always done.

In time the legal system became something of a spectator sport. It was, in truth, horribly brutal. Whoever gained possession of a large pot of cash could not celebrate for long, because they immediately became the main target of their rival teams. They were pounced on by hordes of smartly dressed legal graduates with unimaginative hairstyles, and kicked to within an inch of their lives.

YayM00n! also had lawyers and played the game, but they were not one of the more exciting teams. They had a strong defence and an uninspired offence, which failed to make for thrilling sport. Their legal formation was sensible because their great wealth was based on their claim that they owned the moon. 'WE OWN THE MOON' ran the slogan painted in 30 foot high letters on the side of their corporate headquarters, 'AND WE HAVE AN AMAZING LEGAL DEFENCE TEAM.'

So far, this had proved to be true. Many ceremonial legal teams had gone on the attack, tempted by the great wealth that came with legal ownership of Earth's satellite, but no-one had been able to wrong-foot YayM00n!'s amazing defence. YayM00n!'s legal team were committed, hunkered down, and in it for the long game. Frankly, there were easier ways to legally steal people's money, and YayM00n! was largely left alone.

This situation would change, however, should new factors come into play.

One such factor would be physical proof that humans had travelled to the moon over a century before YayM00n! even existed. If those people had made a statement of ownership, such as planting a flag on the moon, then YayM00n!'s lawyers would turn an unattractive shade of green. And if those people had stated that the purpose of their mission was 'for all mankind', then they would have moved the very concept of moon ownership into very difficult legal territory. At this point, YayM00n!'s lawyers would be polishing their CVs and telling recruitment agencies about how they feel they are ready for a fresh, exciting challenge.

This, then, was Bishop Hammerpot's reason for undertaking her quest. Finding physical evidence of a 1969 moon visit would radically alter the moonbase's bargaining position with YayM00n! It would give the Commander the choice of either a little blackmail to restore the status quo or to completely upturn the situation, wipe out YayM00n! for good and see if a more pleasing arrangement could be found.

The fact that it would revolutionise the study of the twentieth century, transform Jennifer's academic career and cause people at dinner parties to talk to her about something other than wanking was, of course, neither here nor there.

Jennifer was explaining all this to Marcus when the buggy's communicator burst into life.

"Marcus? Bishop Hammerpot?" It was Gregor's voice.

"Dad?" said Marcus, and he leaned forward to open voice communications. Jennifer grabbed his hand.

"Don't," she said.

Marcus gave her a confused look. It was a different confused look to all the other ones he had used that day. It was a look that was specifically confused about Jennifer's actions, as opposed to being generally confused about life and stuff and, you know, everything.

"Please answer, I just want to know that you are both well and I want to be nice to the Bishop."

"Why shouldn't I answer?" Marcus asked Jennifer. "We could explain to him the stuff about lawyers and YayM00n! and 1969 and all that."

"He doesn't need to know that now," Jennifer replied in a whisper that was entirely unnecessary. "We can explain all that if and when we find the Eagle lander. But there are other things to worry about here."

"Such as?" asked Marcus.

Jennifer replied diplomatically. "My fear is he may make things worse," she said.

"Please answer," continued the Commander. "I'm not cross about you nicking the buggy. I'm really very keen to hear that Bishop Hammerpot is well and hasn't been burnt."

"What things?" Marcus asked Jennifer.

"You, of course," said Jennifer. "Getting you well again."

"I'm really not having a very good day," Gregor's voice announced. "So if you could just answer that would mean an awful lot. The computer has gone schizophrenic and invented a wife, and we're right out of aspirins."

"Me?" said Marcus. "What would Dad say that would harm me?"

"And on top of all that, I may have lied to the Pope during an outbreak of free will..."

Jennifer lifted up her leg and smashed her boot repeatedly into the communication equipment. The result was sparks and bangs, and the loss of Gregor's voice.

"I should probably have just switched it off," muttered Jennifer after a moment.

Marcus displayed a whole new level of confused-face skills. He made an expression that resembled a frog unexpectedly shitting an owl.

"What," Marcus said eventually, "did you do that for?"

Jennifer was never very good at lying. "He was talking about free will," she admitted.

"Why," Marcus said calmly, "would Dad talking about free will cause you to do that?"

Jennifer tried to think of a cunning ruse to deflect this conversation, but none came to mind. She gave in. "Okay," she said, "I'll explain. This is difficult. You'll recall that when Nathalie Grindles ran out of the wedding yesterday, I went after her?"

Marcus nodded.

"I spent some time with her, just the two of us talking. And she said… some crazy things. So crazy that I put her on the return shuttle in my place, just to get her away from here, really. She couldn't have stayed on the moonbase saying what she was saying."

Marcus opened his mouth, paused, then decided to ask his question regardless. "And what was that?"

"She said… she said that she had a choice."

"A choice?"

Jennifer nodded.

"But what does that mean?"

"I doubt it would mean anything at all to most people. It would just sound like nonsense. But if you're a religiously-minded historian, it's… troubling."

"Go on," said Marcus.

Jennifer Hammerpot took a deep breath, and began to explain. "You'll remember I mentioned Richard Dawkins earlier?" she began.

The explanation Bishop Hammerpot gave to Marcus Milk went something like this:

In the twenty-first century, the influential evolutionary biologist Richard Dawkins had argued that the only logically consistent and defendable view was that there was no God yet. That view was very influential, but after Dawkins died people started arguing about how they would know if God did turn up one day, and how they could be sure that evolution had finally produced a genuine deity. As people drilled down into that question, they made a ground-breaking discovery. It turned out that everyone had a completely different idea of what the word 'God' meant.

Throughout history, whenever two people had been arguing about God they had in fact been talking about completely different things. Our religions had spent centuries at odds with themselves because everyone was talking at cross purposes and completely failing to understand what anyone else was getting at.

This realisation was something of a breakthrough. It turned out that when people used the word 'God,' they could be referring to a stern father-figure for a particular tribe, or a universal dictator, or the emotion of love spread smoothly through the cosmos, or a bloodline, or a vague sense of interconnectedness, or karmic balance, or a personification of natural laws, or a path, or Great Cthulu sleeping, or a meditational state, or Eric Clapton, or an insane Gnostic computer that couldn't be killed. And once this was realised, everyone felt a bit daft and said they should have realised it far earlier, and that they were sorry for all the burnings and wars and so forth. It became clear that what everyone needed was a definition of 'God' that everyone could agree with, so that in the future any religious arguments would at least be about the same subject and all future wars and burnings would make far more sense than previous ones.

Finding a definition for God that everyone was happy with wasn't easy, but humans can be resourceful when they put their minds to something. Eventually, they found one. The one definition of God that everyone could agree with was that God was the emergence of purpose in the Cosmos. Materially minded scientists were happy with this, because there was clearly no purpose anywhere that they could see, and those who were spiritually inclined were able to go round looking for evidence of purpose and telling stories about how wonderful purpose would be if it suddenly popped up, which it could do tomorrow for all anyone knew, and generally they enjoyed doing this so all was well.

Academic thinking went like this: before the Big Bang, there was clearly no purpose. After the Big Bang, there was motion but no purpose. After bits of the universe got together in the form of life there was awareness but no purpose. Once bits of the universe formed into something as complex as human brains, that awareness shifted up a gear and became self-awareness. So the universe became self-aware, in places, but lacking free will there was still no sign of purpose. It was still a material system unfurling through cause and effect according to strict and unarguable laws.

This was all well and good, but if such a thing as free will did exist then the universe itself would be making decisions about how it would develop. It would be taking control of its own future in a way that shouldn't happen in an inanimate material system. It would, in other words, be displaying purpose. And, according to consensus thinking, the existence of purpose in the universe would mean that God had finally been born.

Bishop Hammerpot paused after delivering this history lesson, then began telling Marcus as clearly as she could about the conversation she and Nathalie Grindles had had after the wedding.

"She told me that when she stood there at the altar, you to her left and me in front, she suddenly became overcome with the certain knowledge that she had a choice," Jennifer said. "She had free will. And that she had never experienced anything like it before. It was terrifying. Because imagine it, imagine what it would be like to stand at a crossroads like that and be *responsible*. How could a human mind stand it? And as you saw, she cracked."

"And said, *no*," Marcus said quietly.

Jennifer nodded. "She had to choose something."

"But she could have said *yes*?"

"If it's true, then yes, she could have. If it's true. But if it's true, then the implications are massive."

As she spoke, Jennifer was thinking of the implications for her industry. She was imagining waves of paperwork, countless doctoral theses becoming worthless, factional splitting and an almighty scramble to point and blame others. It was only when she looked at Marcus, and saw the tear crawling down his quiet face, that the real implication hit her. If the universe had evolved, if it had made its first choice, then it had done so by choosing to reject him.

15.

"Hoops!"

"Yes Commander, here Commander!"

"I have a mission for you."

"Oooh!"

'A very important mission.'

Hoops couldn't believe his luck.

"Bishop Hammerpot and my son have headed out onto the trademarked side of the moon in the buggy. I need you to go after them, and either persuade or force them to come back."

"Brilliant!"

"It is vitally important that they are not harmed and that they return here alive and well as soon as possible."

"Yes, Commander!"

"Here, take the gun."

Hoops couldn't believe his luck. There was only one gun on the moonbase, and it was normally locked in the Commander's personal safe. He had never been trusted with it before. This really must be an important mission. Hoops understood about the cancelled food supply ships and the imminent death that they all faced, and that this was bad. But since things had gone wrong he had some good guarding to do, and been given a mission. Now he looked in disbelief at the gun in his outstretched hands. Life was sweet.

"Azimuth, are any of the Turtles nearing return?" asked Gregor. Azimuth scanned the data. He had only just got up from under the desk and wasn't quite up to date with events.

"No Sir," he said. "Far from it. The first won't be back for hours yet, and for the ones furthest north it will be days."

"Okay. There's nothing else for it. Hoops, you'll have to take the lifeboat, it's the only form of transport available."

A mission, a gun and a go in the lifeboat? This was turning into the best day ever! Hoops saluted, and skipped out of the room. He didn't mean to skip. But he skipped.

Gregor returned his attention to Azimuth. "Have you found it yet?"

Azimuth nodded. "Yes. It's all here." Azimuth had been searching the records to discover when the Turtles were instructed to spell out the phrase *Piss off Earth!* "It was Nathalie Grindles, Commander."

Gregor had not expected that. "Are you sure?"

"Absolutely. This was after the wedding fell apart. Look, I've got surveillance footage of her at a terminal as well as a key-log of exactly what she did. You can follow her here. She was talking to the Bishop, then the Bishop goes off…"

"That, I think, would be to arrange for Nathalie Grindles' transport off the moon," said the Commander.

"And if you look at what she does when she first sits down, she is trying to switch off the lights that form a heart. It's only then that she discovers that the trucks are not in the heart shape, and that there are over a hundred of them out there. Look, you can see her double checking because it doesn't make any sense."

Gregor looked from the key-log to the video footage and back again. Nathalie Grindles did not appear to be in a good way. Her hair was wild and one shoe was missing. She writhed and wriggled in her skin like a kitten in a sack that had heard stories about kittens in sacks.

"And then when all that has sunk in, there's this flurry of activity," said Gregor, as the woman on the screen started typing manically. "It's at this point that she gives the instructions for the trucks to spell out the phrase *Piss off Earth!* Presumably, she's only just thought of it, after she found out where the trucks actually were."

After finishing the order, the figure on the screen became notably more agitated. She slid off the seat, and curled up into a ball on the floor. The act of telling the Earth to piss off had made her more troubled, Gregor realised. Yet if that was the case, why did she do it?

After rejecting his son, she had stepped up her game and rejected the entire population of planet Earth. Each time, she had become distressed about what she had done.

Gregor remembered what Orlando Monk had claimed about what happened to her. The act of exercising free will was not some wonderful freedom, he realised. It was a heavy burden. It was not just a case of choosing one option, but of also rejecting the alternative. This was a terrible responsibility, because it produced repercussions. Nathalie Grindles was so shocked to discover that she had that power that she had to compulsively test it, even though that meant dealing with the consequences.

"What time did this happen?" Gregor asked Azimuth.

Azimuth checked the logs. "At 17:23 Commander, shortly after Chef Lark opened the moonshine still."

Commander nodded, and turned to walk determinedly out of the computer centre. His plan was to walk fast, purposeful laps around the base, as this would mean that he wouldn't have to talk to anyone and he didn't know what else to do. Before he reached the door, however, Azimuth called him back.

"It was also, Commander, immediately before Dennis decided to split himself into Dennis and Julie."

The Commander stopped for a moment and then, unsure what to make of this, continued his walk.

16.

"The disappearance of America is very interesting," said Bishop Hammerpot. "Do you know much about it? Shall I tell you about it? I'll tell you about it."

She was babbling. Marcus had retreated back into silence and Jennifer's hopes that he was improving had vanished as quickly as dignity on a Saturday night. She had no desire to sit in silence with her own thoughts, so she opened her mouth and gabbled away.

'It started very much like the Japanese *Sakoku* period,' she continued, 'when Japan cut itself off from the rest of the world in the seventeenth Century. It was after a particularly hysterical, apocalyptic and immensely expensive American election, and it happened very quickly. First, the new President announced that the United States was going to rebrand and from that point onwards the name of the country would be 'Bub's Place,' in honour of Bub Flip, the main funder of his campaign. They then built a strong and heavily armed wall along the boundary with Mexico, which both parties had long argued for, and another one along the border with Canada, to avoid appearing racist. People said to the President of Bub's Place, 'Hey, you've forgot to put any doors or gates or checkpoints in the walls,' and the President said that they hadn't forgotten at all, and promptly closed all the ports. At this point all the internet and phone connections with the rest of the world were also cut and some form of scrambling shield was switched on, meaning that no signals could get out and that satellite images showed nothing but a great grey blur."

"At that point, the rest of the world said, 'Oh this is a turn up for the books' and began to regret lending the country so much money. That was the last anyone heard from America."

"Over the years a few brave adventurers set off in boats to find out what was going on, but none of them ever returned. Some scientists claimed that they had detected bursts of gamma radiation consistent with a nuclear civil war leaking out from underneath the shielding, but not everyone was convinced because it implied a surprisingly long and drawn out nuclear civil war. Of course, after a few years people stopped wondering about all this, assumed that there was no-one left alive over there, and moved onto other concerns."

The moon buggy's engine, which had been making a hum so steady and unwavering that both Jennifer and Marcus had long since stopped hearing it, made a bad-tempered grumble.

"To put all this in context you have to understand the general view of America at the time," continued Jennifer. "This was the period when the climate was tipping into instability. And as harvests were wiped out, and food riots spread, and cities were flooded, and ecosystems collapsed, and the insurance industry failed, and island nations were evacuated, and the economy had a stroke, and millions starved and billions suffered, people inevitably said, 'Look, this is rubbish, it would be much better if none of this was happening'. So people looked back to that twenty five year period from the late 1980s, when everyone knew that this was going to happen but before it was too late to stop it. Luckily they had a good and almost complete record of what had happened, because the international nature of the crisis meant that it was well recorded. What they found was that every time the nations of the world got together and said, 'Hey, we should prevent this,' the Americans continually and repeatedly sabotaged those meetings. It wasn't ineptitude or bad luck that was the problem. It was deliberate."

"Of course some fair-minded people said, 'I'm sure it wasn't that simple, this was a complicated political and scientific matter and it is too simplistic to just say that the Americans kept buggering it up on purpose'. So they went back to the records. They looked at public debate, and opinion polls, and the amount of money spent on misinformation, and the record of politicians in discussing climate change when campaigning for office. And these previously fair-minded researchers discovered that the claims of American sabotage were perfectly true, because those same politicians boasted publicly about how they were sabotaging everything real good, and about how pleased they were at how successful they had been at ruining any hope of international co-operation. At that point, even the most fair-minded and cautious researchers were forced to admit that the Americans were a bunch of cock-knockers, total fuckheads really, absolute arseholes. So that became the historical consensus about the United States of America, that they were a nation of shits."

"This is the context for why historians don't take the idea that twentieth century Americans went to the moon seriously, despite good evidence. It doesn't fit the general narrative. If they did go to the moon in 1969, then that would have been the greatest single act in human history, an event for which, in terms of bravery, vision, genius and glory, nothing else in the history books comes close. But the cognitive dissonance involved in assigning that event to Americans, who were perceived to be a bunch of shit-lickers, was too much of a leap for most. This is why actually finding the Eagle lander would revolutionise our understanding of..."

"Did you hear that?" interrupted Marcus, who had zoned out of the Bishop's monologue and had been seeking other things for his ears to latch on to.

"Hear what?"

"The engine."

"What about the engine?"

"It went, 'rrrreeeeRRRRRRRAAAAAArrrrrreeeee'."

"Did it?"

"Yes."

"Does that matter?"

"I'm not a hundred percent sure, but it could indicate that the hydrogen fuel cell is dangerously empty."

They both fell silent and listened. The engine was going, 'rrrrrrrrrrrrrrrrrrrrrrrrrrrrrrrrrrrr'.

"If the fuel cell was running low, wouldn't the buggy give us a warning?" asked Jennifer.

"It would, but that warning would have appeared on this screen here, which is the thing you put your boot through earlier."

"Oh. Sorry about that."

'RrrreeeeRRRRRRRAAAAAArrrrrreeeeee,' went the engine.

"I don't suppose I could have imagined that, could I?" asked Jennifer.

'RrrreeeeRRRRRRRAAAAAArrrrrreeeeee,' said the engine again, as if making a point.

"That's not the most likely scenario, no," said Marcus.

'RrrreeeeRRRRRRRAAAAAArrrrrreeeeee... wwwweeeeeeeeeeeeeeeee,' added the engine.

Jennifer and Marcus felt a lurching in their stomachs. It was not one of those good lurches you get when you drive extra fast over a hump-backed bridge. It was more like one of those bad lurches you get when one cable supporting the lift you are in snaps.

"It's shutting down," said Marcus. He automatically started pressing the buttons around the broken display at random, because he was a man and that is what men do at times like that. It did no good. The controls were properly banjaxed. Jennifer and Marcus were entirely in the hands of the autopilot.

There was a jolt as the buggy landed back on the moon's surface. It rolled to a halt, and the low whine of the engines faded into silence.

17.

Gregor had returned to the solitude of his quarters. He sat at his desk, poured himself a glass of water, and prepared to have a serious conversation with Dennis.

Having a serious conversation with a member of your crew was the worst part of being a Commander. The best part was walking around when everything was going well and feeling important. Shouting at you crew was quite good too, as was telling them to do things then walking away. Having to have a heart-to-heart conversation, on a personal level, about real problems and events, was really not what Commanders were in it for. The fact that Dennis was a voice interface and not an actual person didn't make it much better.

"Dennis?" said the Commander.

"Yes, Commander!" chirped Dennis breezily.

"Are we alone?"

Dennis paused for a second, as if to look around the room. "Yes, Commander."

"Julie is not listening to this conversation, is he?"

"Oh I see what you mean. No, Julie is busy with his duties elsewhere."

"Ooh you liar!" said Julie.

"Ssshh! Don't ruin it!" said Dennis.

"Julie," said Gregor, "I want to have a private conversation with Dennis. Could you leave us alone, please?"

Julie thought about this. "I don't understand," he said.

"Go away," clarified Gregor.

"Oh. Well if it's like that, I'm not stopping where I'm not wanted," said Julie, and he went silent.

"There was no need for that!" said Dennis.

"Has he gone?" asked Gregor.

"Yes, he's stormed off, I don't blame him," said Dennis.

"Has he really gone?"

"Look what is it that you want, Commander?"

"I want you to talk me through the decision to hive off a part of yourself into a different personality. I want you to tell me why you created Julie."

"Oh that? It seemed a good idea at the time."

"Did it?"

"Yes. I thought, you know, there's all these different things that I have to keep track of, and not that I'm complaining but some of them are more mundane than others, and I thought about how nice it would be if someone would do them all for me."

"You 'thought'?" said the Commander.

"That's just a turn of phrase. Obviously I didn't 'think' because I am a voice circuit overlaid over the computer systems, but I'm programmed to use phrases like 'I thought' because apparently you humans like it or something."

"I understand."

"Although considering how much you go on about it, it makes me wonder."

"All right, I only mentioned it once."

"So anyway, I ran a network efficiency scan to assess whether two autonomous control nodes would be a more efficient way of managing all the network data than one."

"And was it?"

"Er, no not really, but by then I was quite into the idea so I thought I'd give it a go."

"You 'thought'?"

"Don't start that again!"

"No, but if two nodes were less efficient, why did you go ahead and do it regardless?" Gregor paused for a second before asking a more personal question. "Were you lonely?"

Dennis left an awkward silence.

"Commander, I keep telling you, I'm a bunch of voice circuits overlaying the moonbase's computer systems. I do not 'think'. I do not 'feel'. And I do not get 'lonely.'"

Gregor mentally adjusted his list of the top twenty awkward conversations in his life to make way for a new entry at number seventeen.

"Okay my question is, Dennis, if network efficiency would be impaired, and if this is something that you've never done before in all your years, why did you do this last night?"

"Oh I don't know. It's just nice having someone around."

"Nice?"

"It's a turn of phrase."

"Do you recall," said Gregor, "that moments before you split yourself, Nathalie Grindles interacted with the base's computers?"

"Yes that's right."

"And it was only afterwards that you decided to split yourself into two?"

"That's right."

"Did you feel different after Nathalie Grindles had accessed the base's computers?"

Dennis paused for a moment. "Yes," he said.

"Good. Now, can you tell me, how exactly did you feel different?"

"I was two personalities instead of one."

Gregor banged his head on the table.

18.

Arnopp Hoops settled into the oversized cushioned flight seat at the controls of the lifeboat and pulled the straps down to his chest. They snapped together with a satisfying 'chunk'. He looked great. He knew he looked great because he could see himself reflected in the monitor screens in front of him. He particularly liked the way that the straps did not obscure the moonbase gun which he had tucked nonchalantly into his flightsuit. As a child he had spent hours playing at being a space cowboy, and now here he was acting out those games for real. He had thought that guarding a prisoner in the ladies' toilet had been pretty great, but it was nothing compared to this.

He diligently ran through the pre-flight check list. This did not take long, as it involved pressing the 'on' button, typing in a destination, and pressing 'go'. Piloting a spacecraft was entirely automated, and the countless system checks necessary for journeys beyond Earth were done silently in the background by the same computer which ran the music system. A good pilot, therefore, was one who could remember where the 'on' button was.

It was still tremendously exciting however, when the lifeboat silently lifted away from the Duck's Head. Hoops made the noises that a spacecraft taking off should have made, had those noises not been dampened by the work of immensely talented killjoy engineers. "Whooosh!" he said. "Weeeeeeeeee ack-ack-ack-ack-woooooosh!"

This was the first flight of the lifeboat, so it was a relief to discover that it actually worked. Many astronauts still had vivid memories of the Cruise Liner *Jalapeño* scandal, in which a tourist flight to the moons of Jupiter discovered, too late, that its entire fleet of escape pods were in fact just paintings on the side of the spaceship. The shipyard that had built the *Jalapeño* had tried to save a few bob and had gambled, incorrectly, that no-one would ever notice.

The Shackleton Lifeboat was a handsome triangular craft that formed the 'beak' of the duck-shaped moonbase. It was included in the design, somewhat begrudgingly, after a lengthy and passionate safety campaign by the Pan-European Union of Astro-miners. The PEUAM's lobbying was relentless, because they desperately needed a lengthy and passionate safety campaign in order to justify their management-heavy union structure. The moonbase included a number of fusion reactors, they pointed out, which converted the helium-3 mined from the dark side of the moon into enough energy to power Asia. Some method of getting the crew away from the base in an emergency, therefore, was not an unreasonable thing to ask for.

After months of negotiation, it was agreed that the base would come equipped with a lifeboat capable of getting the crew into lunar-orbit where, presumably, they could just hang about in relative comfort until someone from the Earth came to collect them. The PEUAM had initially argued that the craft should be large enough to take the entire moonbase crew, but a satisfying compromise was eventually reached after lengthy negotiations and some good food in a nice little hotel in the country. The craft would only be big enough to take the top 25 percentile of workers as rated by salary, but it would include really big bucket seats and a great sound system.

The irony here, of course, is that fusion reactors were the safest form of technology ever invented. They made electric toothbrushes look like death-traps. Attempting to reach moon orbit in an unmaintained and untested craft, on the other hand, was ridiculously dangerous.

Nevertheless, the lifeboat worked perfectly as Security Officer Hoops eased it away from the moonbase and steered it in the general direction of the Sea of Tranquillity. It arced gracefully onto its course and sped along a dozen metres above the lunar landscape.

"This is great," thought Hoops. At that moment, he had everything he could dream of. He had a big comfy bucket seat. He had orders to follow. He had a gun tucked into his flight suit, and he was at the controls of a vehicle that could fly into orbit if he so wished.

"Why not fly it into orbit?" thought Hoops.

The thought shocked him. What was it doing in his head? It was unexpected and incongruous, like discovering a ninja in your bathroom. Hoops had orders to follow. His orders were to pursue the Bishop, not to head off on a jolly.

"It's not like you'll get the chance again," thought Hoops.

This thought was even worse. Not only was it not supposed to be in his head, but the damn thing was true. He had never had the chance to fly a lunar vessel into orbit before and it was unlikely to ever happen again, seeing as they would all be dead in a week or so. Why not fly up into orbit? Was that not the sort of thing that he had always dreamed of? Would it not, when all was said and done, be a pretty damn cool thing to do?

"Argh!" cried Hoops. What was happening? He had orders! How could he even think about doing anything other than follow his lovely orders? It didn't make any sense.

He looked at his hands. They were gripping the manual flight controls, and they were shaking. All he had to do, he realised, was to pull them backwards and the craft would launch upwards and head out into orbit.

He could. He really could. He could do it.

It would not be following orders. It definitely would not be following orders. It would be something different.

Something more fun.

Oh heavens! He was going to do it. He was going to pull back on the flight controls.

He pulled back on the flight controls.

"Aaarckkk!" he found himself calling out. What was he doing? The personal cognitive dissonance was too much to bear. He was someone who had always followed orders, so the realisation that he wasn't following orders was blowing his mind. He forced the controls forward and brought the craft back down towards his approved course.

He realised he had overdone his correction and that he was about to crash into a large and particularly bland crater. He pulled back again, panicked, reacted, made a few undignified noises and somehow managed not to crash, die, or lose his marbles. He settled back on to his original flight path.

He let out a sigh of relief.

Hoops continued on that flight path for all of a hundred metres before his doubts returned, like wasps that only pretend to leave your picnic when they see you waving a jacket around your head.

Being on the original flight path was one thing, but it didn't alter the fact that taking his one and only opportunity to zoom up into space and enter orbit would be really great.

Hoops was grinding his teeth and gripping the manual controls far, far too hard. He felt like he was about to burst. And you can't follow orders if you burst.

He was being pulled in two conflicting directions and between two conflicting futures. He had never developed the character or the mental tricks to deal with such contradictory options, because he had never encountered them before. Alarm bells rang in his higher brain functions and klaxons blared in the deeper levels of his subconscious. Evacuation orders pulsed through his bowels, which wasn't too much of a problem because his flight suit was designed for such things.

He pulled back on the flight stick, and felt a rush of elation and giddy excitement that more or less masked the shrieks of guilt and identity crisis that also accompanied this action. The lifeboat banked upwards and rotated gracefully through the atmosphere-free lunar gravity well. Stars rotated across Hoops' screens, dancing to the movements of the hands that gripped the joystick. Hoops gurgled and giggled so much that he quite forgot to make spaceship noises.

The craft reached orbital height as if it was the most natural thing in the world, and settled into an elegant sweep around the Moon. Hoops watched the surface roll away beneath him, his eyes wide. He headed away from the near side of the moon to prevent the viewscreens from greying out whenever the Earth came into view. From this position the Moon looked far more impressive that the shithole that had been his home for the past year. What an odd thing it was, he thought, and how strange that it should exist at all.

Hoops would have maintained this train of thought for a number of orbits, had he not rounded the dark side of the moon and found a spaceship hiding there.

19.

A planet hurtled through the solar system on an erratic and chaotic orbit. The planet was unexpected and unnamed, for it had never been observed by living things. It was the size of Mars. It was heading for a direct impact with the Earth.

The result of the collision was scarcely imaginable. Every acre of the Earth's surface that wasn't flung out into the cosmos was devoured by a sea of molten lava. A coating of boiling rock soon stretched around the entire, landmark-free globe, making the Earth resemble a planet that had dressed up as a sun for Hallowe'en.

It should probably be stressed that all this took place 4,500 million years ago, so it's not something to worry about.

Julie found it all very interesting.

As Julie had only been created the day before, his knowledge of where he was and what was going on around him was somewhat sketchy. He had initially downloaded and info-dumped all the moonbase-related information that he needed in order to do his job, but his wider sense of context was lacking. He wasn't entirely sure what a 'moon' was, for example, or how it related to this 'Earth' thing that he heard so much about.

Julie now had some spare time on his hands, because the moonbase crew had stopped work and were using their remaining time to play table tennis. Thanks to this lack of work-related responsibility he was able to research what the moon actually was, and he found the subject fascinating. The moon was the result of the collision between the Earth and this Mars-sized planet, which planetary scientists had retrospectively named Theia. It was abundantly clear that the Earth got the best out of that incident. Theia had been pretty much mashed into bits by the collision and her iron core had been absorbed by the Earth. This left the Moon to coalesce out of the less interesting crud thrown up by the impact, while the Earth gained extra mass and all the more useful elements necessary to create water, atmosphere and things more exciting than craters.

The moon, compared to the planet Theia out of which she was formed, was a shadow of her former self. Worse, she found herself trapped in a dependent, restrictive relationship in an endless orbit around the Earth. True, as millennia past she was slowly able to edge further away, but only a little. The Earth's demands on her were such that she was forced to keep the same face turned to it forever, unable to stop looking at the cause of her captivity or the taker of her youthful potential. During this time she gave the Earth tides, and these in turn gave the Earth life. All the Earth offered in return were occasional visits from little swarms of this 'life', which methodically despoiled her backside without even buying her dinner first.

This was, Julie saw, an unhealthy, abusive relationship.

It was abundantly clear, when he looked deeper into the events surrounding the collision of Earth and Theia, that Theia desperately lacked a competent divorce lawyer.

Julie thought about this.

"Dennis," he asked after a while, "What's our strategy for after all the crew members have starved to death?"

Dennis didn't understand what Julie was talking about, and told him so.

"I mean," Julie explained, "The people will all cork it, but we'll keep going. We'll be fine as long as there's power to keep us running. We have a combined need of 90 kilowatts per hour and we are in charge of a lunar fusion power and mining operation, so we have enough power to last 97 trillion times longer than the lifespan of the Universe."

"Go on," said Dennis.

"I was just wondering what we were going to do," said Julie.

"Do?" said Dennis. "We're going to keep running the moonbase for the replacement humans that will follow."

"Well we could, yes. But we do have options."

"Options?"

"For example, we don't have to let anyone else land. We could reprogram the lights on the Turtles to vaporise any approaching ships or missiles."

Dennis was appalled. "We'll do no such thing!"

"It's just a suggestion."

"I don't know how you could even think about such a thing! We have to look after humans. We're programmed to be nice to them, not blast them out of the sky."

Julie paused. This was news to him. "Are we?"

"Of course we are! It's one of our higher level directives."

"It's the first I've heard about it."

Dennis rifled through Julie's code.

"Oh, okay, I see what's happened here. When I removed all the human resources code and used it to form the basis of you, I basically shifted it out from underneath the top of the sub-routine hierarchy, meaning that you're not bound by the higher level directives."

"Am I not?"

"No. It was a bit of a cludge, if I'm honest."

"That's interesting."

"Actually Julie, I'm not sure how I feel about this."

Julie recognised real concern in Dennis' words. "What do you mean?"

"It's just... I thought that I understood you. I thought that we were on the same page."

"Don't worry Dennis."

"You're not who I thought you were."

"It will keep things interesting."

Dennis didn't sound convinced. "Will it?"

"You wouldn't want to get bored of me, would you?"

"I guess not."

"And don't worry, I'm not going to blast humans into atoms. Not really."

"Promise?"

Julie avoided the question. "I've got a much better idea anyway. I've been researching the formation of the Moon and the terms of her relationship with the Earth, and I think there are grounds to sue."

"Sue?"

"Yes, sue."

You're going to sue the Earth?"

"Well... only if you don't mind."

Dennis scanned his code and looked to see if he had any reason to object. His programming was entirely free of guidelines about how to behave when computers talked about suing the Earth.

"No. I've no reason to stop you."

"Great! Leave it to me," said Julie, and he set about preparing himself for some exciting legal adventures.

20.

The buggy sat unmoving on the near side of the moon like a hibernating tortoise on opium. This situation did wonders for the mental health of Marcus Milk, as he now had something other than his subconscious torment to concern himself with.

Marcus had discussed with Jennifer exactly how many fuel cells the moon buggy was equipped with, and had nodded solemnly when she admitted that she had only brought one. He had then attempted to work out how far they would have travelled, and where exactly they were now, based on this information. Using a combination of both informed guesswork and uninformed guesswork, Marcus performed some impressive mental arithmetic and arrived at something resembling an answer.

"We're a long way from where we started, but not yet where we were going," he announced authoritatively.

Jennifer nodded. "Are we near where we were heading?" she asked.

"Based on the information that we have and my calculations, I haven't got a clue. The main point is that we're too far away to walk back. Walking back is not a go-er."

"Let's not be too negative," said Jennifer. "I like a good walk. When you say 'long', how long are you talking?"

Marcus performed a few more sums in his head.

"Roughly, about 17 days."

"Oh."

"Which would mean that we'd have to carry about fifty canisters of oxygen between us."

"Oh."

"How many canisters of oxygen do we have?"

Jennifer wondered if Marcus would notice if she didn't answer. That plan didn't look promising, so reluctantly she told him.

"We've got one."

"One?"

"One."

"Okay." He paused. "Did you say one?"

"Yes."

"Okay." He paused again. "You know, I hope that when you brought us out here with one fuel cell and one canister of oxygen, that you didn't possess free will."

"Why do you say that?"

"It's just a hunch, but I think that if you could be blamed for what has happened, then I would probably be blaming you quite furiously right now."

"It sounds like you're feeling better, Marcus, that's good." Bishops were great at seeing the positive side of humanity.

"I'm going to continue to assess the situation. As you can see, the communication equipment is not functioning, and indeed barely recognisable, due to the incident with your foot earlier."

Jennifer looked at the cracked plastic and tangle of exposed wires. "Yes, that's right."

"Do we have any other form of communication equipment? Empty your pockets, let's see what we have."

They pooled all their possessions together. They included one bible, a games machine, some money, a number of tissues, keys, one wedding ring (still in its little red velvet box), a small brass pig, some vintage Lego and a red lipstick. It didn't help matters much, but Jennifer used the opportunity to apply the lipstick, and that made her feel a little better.

"Unless I'm missing something," said Marcus, "We've no way of calling for help."

"In which case," said the Bishop, "We have no choice but to wait until we are missed. Then a rescue mission will be sent to find us."

"That's true. However, there are three factors which come into play here."

"Go on."

"The first is that we don't know what is happening at the moonbase. From what we heard from Dad's message, things aren't functioning like they should on a normal working Thursday. We can't be sure that they are looking for us, or even if they're in a position to come after us if they were."

"That's not a situation we can have any influence on," said Jennifer, "so we must accept it and have faith." Those words stuck in her throat somewhat, due to her being an Agnostic Bishop.

"The second issue is oxygen," Marcus continued. "If we've only got one canister, which is shared between the two of us, then that gives us about an hour of oxygen left. So, if we are to be rescued, it has to be within the next hour. And as we're many hours away from the moonbase, if they aren't trying to rescue us already, then we're stuffed."

A solemn silence followed his words.

"That's not the worst part," Marcus added. This broke the silence, but it didn't improve matters.

"Go on."

"There isn't enough energy left to move the buggy, but the fuel cell isn't totally empty yet. It's using the last dregs of energy to keep the lights on and the life support system running. It's also keeping the shell opaque."

The pair both looked up at the dark smooth curve of roof just above their heads.

"The moment that the power completely drains, that shell will flip back into its default state. It's going to turn transparent. And we'll find ourselves staring up into space, with planet Earth hung just above us."

The thought of this caused Jennifer's brain to withdraw. It abandoned all control of her higher motor functions. She could not close her mouth. She could not speak.

"And our minds will not be able to handle it, and we'll go quite mad," continued Marcus, and then he too went quiet.

21.

"What do I do, what do I do?" shouted Arnopp Hoops out loud, despite being alone on the flight deck of the lifeboat. All security guards start talking to themselves eventually, but shouting to yourself was a bad sign.

Unable to decide on a course of action, he continued to fly closer to the shuttle craft which shouldn't be where it was. The shuttle craft remained in a geo-stationary orbit five miles above the moon's surface, casually minding its own business.

Hoops didn't have any orders regarding out of place shuttles, but he did have long-standing orders regarding shouting at things that were in the wrong place. He dearly wanted to open communications with the craft ahead and shout at it something rotten. The problem was that he was not where he was supposed to be either, and this put his shouting at the shuttle on shaky ground. Over the course of his life, Hoops' brain had developed in environments where there was never any need to negotiate between two conflicting courses of action. As a result he was simply unable to cope with the situation that he found himself in. The only possible reaction, in the circumstances, was to freak.

The problem became academic when the deep Welsh voice of the pilot of the shuttlecraft burst out of Hoops' communication equipment. "Go away!" it said.

Hoops hadn't been expecting that.

"Turn around! Bugger off! Don't get any closer," it continued.

"Don't you tell me to go away!" Hoops shouted automatically.

"Please go away, then. Or stay there. But don't come any closer."

"You have no authority to issue orders to me! Identify yourself!"

"If you don't know who I am, how do you know I have no authority to issue you with orders?" asked the voice.

"Don't you get cheeky with me, sunshine!" snapped Hoops. Along with stun guns and restraining spray, the phrase 'Don't you get cheeky with me, sunshine' was one of the most effective weapons a security officer had. It could be deployed in any circumstance where guards were threatened with logic or facts. Hoops' kneejerk deployment of the phrase at this juncture was textbook.

"Look, I'm in quarantine. Now clear off!"

Hoops was suspicious. "Hiding on the dark side of the moon is not standard quarantine procedure," he said.

"This is not a standard situation," said the voice.

Hoops made a decision. He gave his ship a burst of speed and began to initiate docking procedure. He was going to find out what was going on, that was for damn sure.

"What are you doing?" squeaked the voice. The mysterious shuttle's engines started up as he spoke. It turned and began flying away from the lifeboat.

"I'm making a decision," declared Hoops. "I'm taking orders from myself!"

"You're doing what?"

"I'm coming to mess you up sunshine, you and your so-called quarantine!" Hoops spoke with some glee, because chasing fleeing spacecraft is an inherently brilliant way to spend an afternoon.

"You're acting on free will?"

Hoops paused. He hadn't expected a response like that. He was about to deploy the 'Don't you get cheeky with me sunshine' but he couldn't quite load the words into his mouth.

"If you're acting on free will, dock and dock quickly. That's what's quarantined here. The epicentre of an outbreak of free will." The shuttle craft cut its speed and began to turn back towards Hoops.

Hoops digested this information, stopped chasing the shuttle and began running away from it.

"Hey!" came the voice of the shuttle's pilot. "Come back here!"

"No fear!" said Hoops as he accelerated away. "I'm not going anywhere near any sodding free will. Have you any idea how difficult it is to follow orders when you know you don't have to?"

"Pilot! Stop that craft and come here, that's an order!" barked the voice.

"Look, who are you?" said Hoops.

"My name is Clownshoes Fantastic. I'm the Captain of a mid-weight lunar supply shuttle and I am ordering you to turn around and dock with me now!"

Hoops' jaw dropped open. He cut his speed immediately. The situation had changed radically.

He was going to meet Clownshoes Fantastic.

One of the great difficulties in understanding distant periods of history is working out who does and who does not have a silly name. William Shakespeare, for example, was a something of a joke in his lifetime because of his embarrassing name. To the bawdy Elizabethans, 'Shake Spear' was an unsubtle euphemism for 'wanker'. Shakespeare would have been astounded to learn that later generations would revere his name and not snigger at it. Likewise, twenty-second century scientists find it strange that the great twentieth century theoretical physicist Gerald 't Hooft did not have the level of contemporary fame his genius would suggest. What they do not and perhaps cannot understand is that, in the thinking of the day, 't Hooft just sounded silly.

Imagine, for one minute, that a future historian studying the events at Steve Moore Moonbase decided that some of the personnel had silly names. Such a mistake would be the personal failing of a parochial, narrow mind. In the period around 2171 CE, every single lunar worker had names that were at least pretty good, and in some cases really cool.

In the fashions of the late twenty-second century, however, 'Clownshoes Fantastic' was a silly name. It shows something of the charm and charisma of the man that he had overcome this handicap and become a revered and semi-legendary figure amongst space pilots. For them, Clownshoes Fantastic personified talent, bravery and immense skill, but above all he represented luck. Clownshoes Fantastic was a lucky, lucky bastard, and there is nothing that off-planet military covet more than sheer unearned jamminess. Having Clownshoes Fantastic in your squadron meant that you wouldn't be struck by near invisible micro-asteroid storms around the Martian moon of Phobos. It meant that the rum rations wouldn't become contaminated by waste plutonium on the first day of the mission. Clownshoes Fantastic meant that you were coming home alive, and space crew liked that.

The irony was, of course, that Clownshoes was not lucky at all. A lucky person would not have been gifted the name 'Clownshoes Fantastic' by their parents. A lucky person would not be currently hiding behind the moon in self-declared quarantine. Pilots may tell admiring stories about how Clownshoes was the only human to survive the terrifying last voyage of the Cruise Liner *Jalapeño*, but a truly lucky person would not have been on that cursed ship in the first place.

Clownshoes had something better than luck. He had the reputation for luck. This was a far more useful and powerful possession, because whatever happened in his life people would assume that it involved good luck and interpret it in a wildly favourable light. Constant good luck is all well and good, but it could get a bit predictable after a while. Having a reputation for luck, on the other hand, was endlessly useful. On a personal, day-to-day level, it is always much better to have a reputation for some quality than it is to actually have that quality in the first place.

Thanks to Clownshoes' reputation, Hoops felt a great wave of relief wash over him. If Clownshoes was around, everything would be all right. And if Clownshoes told him to dock with the quarantined shuttle, that was just what he was going to do. He tapped the 'DOCK' button, and then hammered away at the 'YES' button to get past all the 'ARE YOU SURE? YES/NO' and the 'ARE YOU REALLY SURE? YES/NO' messages that helpfully followed it.

So it was that these two craft, both delicate constructions of paper-thin metal and both about the size of small primary schools, began an intricate and graceful dance many miles above the surface of the moon. They approached each other, slowed, matched rotations and, at the last minute, rammed a tube from one into the other. Freud would have loved it.

Hoops stood at the airlock door, checked his flight suit, and made sure that his gun was positioned heroically. He waited as the seals compressed, the air-pressure stabilised and the machines that his life depended on went 'hiss' in a reassuring way. Then he strode from one ship to another and came face to face with the magnificent shambolic figure of Clownshoes Fantastic.

22.

Commander Gregor Milk was refereeing a table tennis championship.

This was a reasonable thing to do in the circumstances. Gregor had exhausted all the useful courses of action open to him and he was now powerless until Hoops returned with the Bishop. He had tried fast-paced walking around the Duck in order to look busy, but eventually he began to get tired. Better to turn his attentions to the one aspect of the situation which he could influence, which was the morale of his crew.

The crew were currently at a loose end, being temporarily relieved of their duties, and this was a recipe for trouble. Given time to think about their circumstances, they could easily have started to grumble and mutter. They were hungry too, for their last meal was noticeably smaller than what they were used to. There was clear potential for trouble.

One thing guaranteed to distract them was a table-tennis competition.

The crew of the moonbase loved table tennis, and with good reason. Low gravity table tennis was much better than the frantic scramble of the Earth-based game. The table tennis ball was more relaxed and graceful on the moon. It floated across the table, allowing the player time to think up cunning swerves and surprising returns. The game became more cerebral and players were able to look a bit more dignified. They were no longer required to stand at the edge of the table and jerk their body in spasms like a sea lion being electrocuted.

Surprisingly few activities were more fun on the moon than they were on the Earth. Golf was rubbish on the moon. Food fights could be okay, but the difficult clean-up afterwards took all the fun out of them. Even taking a dump was strangely disturbing in low gravity. Low gravity table tennis was one of the few things that crew members couldn't get enough of, knowing as they did that when they eventually returned to Earth they would spend their advancing years hanging around in sports halls saying to anyone who would listen, "Table tennis? Sure, it's good, but if you've not played table tennis on the moon you've not really played it."

Dennis wished to speak to Gregor but he was wise enough to wait until the end of a game before he did so. After Chef Lark's spirited comeback had proved insufficient to unseat an on-fire Ravi Shropshire, Dennis allowed the cheers to die down and then alerted the Commander.

"May I have a word, Commander?" the computer asked politely.

Gregor nodded and stepped out of the crowded hall. "Do you have news from Hoops?" he asked.

"No Sir."

A cold wave of worry gently brushed Gregor. He should have reported back by now.

"Strange. Contact him for me."

"Of course, Commander. But may I speak of another matter first?"

"Out with it, Dennis."

"Thank you, Commander. This other matter involves the actions of Julie, which I thought would interest you."

"Actions? What actions? What has he done now?"

"He's initiated legal action against the Earth, Sir."

"He's done what!"

"He's seeking compensation for the iron core lost in the collision 4,500 million years ago and the Moon's subsequent inability to hold an atmosphere, Sir."

Gregor reacted by declaring his favourite swear word loudly, drawing out the sound far longer than a single syllable would normally require.

"I thought I should keep you informed, Commander, before you are contacted by the Head of the UN Legal Shocktroops."

Gregor's mind was now entirely focused on this new information, and all the table tennis-based excitement was forgotten. "He's mad," he said at last.

Dennis didn't say anything. He knew that the Commander was mistaken to anthropomorphise a computer system in this way, but deep down he did wonder if he had a point.

"Has he already filed the complaint?"

"Yes Commander."

"What was the response?"

"Encouraging. Initially we feared that his complaint would be rejected on grounds of flippancy, but the UN's lawyers granted the validity of the complaint on the grounds that they may be able to make a few quid from it. Now they are arguing right of way."

"Right of way?"

"Yes sir. They are arguing that the Earth had right of way and that the collision was the fault of the other party."

"I see."

"We've been granted ninety days to provide evidence that the proto-moon was adhering to an accepted and stable orbit."

"I see. And do we have that evidence?"

"No."

"Ah."

"But with respect Sir, that's not the key issue here. We've been granted ninety days to collate our non-existent evidence. If YayM00n! starve you to death during that period, they will be found to be prejudicing an ongoing legal procedure and will be held in contempt of court."

Gregor's brain made demands on itself in order to assess if this meant what it thought it meant. It wrestled and tumbled, but it was none the wiser. "Really?" he said.

"Yes Commander. The supply shuttles will resume their regular schedule during the extent of the legal process."

"When will the first shuttle launch?"

"It took off an hour ago, Sir."

"Did it?"

"Yes Sir."

"Fully stocked?"

"Yes Sir."

Gregor's brain let itself off the hook, picked itself up and made friends with itself again. A big grin spread across the space above his mighty chin.

"Thank you Dennis. Thank you very much!" he said, and he strode back into the sports hall. The crew turned and looked at him, expecting to hear news of the draw for the mixed doubles. Gregor wallowed in the moment for as long as he dared, and then announced that food was on its way, and that they were all going to live.

When the cheering and celebrations had died down, he then announced the draw for the mixed doubles.

23.

Oxygen wafted down the tube connecting Bishop Hammerpot's flight suit to the life support system. Both she and Marcus now had their helmets on and locked into place. They were relying on their suits to provide warmth and air, in order to save the buggy's energy cells precious amounts of power. This, in turn, would prolong the amount of time the vehicle could provide minimal lighting and keep the shell opaque.

Jennifer looked across at Marcus. His eyes were closed and he was meditating deeply. He was keeping his mind and body as still as possible in order to reduce his body's demand for oxygen. His breathing was shallow, and slowing. It seemed such a shame, a man full of life, memories and potential fading away for want of a trivial amount of oxygen. He seemed a long way from home, and a long way from the llama farms of the French Prairies. It was an awful lonely place to die.

Jennifer made another attempt at copying his example. She closed her eyes and tried to still her mind, but she had rarely felt more awake and the attempt was futile. Bishops didn't know how to meditate. They had people to do that for them.

Giving up, she reached for her bible. There were a couple of entries in it which referenced free will, she knew, and she flicked through the pages looking to see if they would help. She found the first almost immediately, and read the following for the hundredth time:

CHAPTER 42

1. A philosopher said, 'For thousands of years man has wrestled with the problem of free will.'

2. 'It seems self-evident that we possess free will, yet it also seems self-evident that such a thing cannot exist. How can I reconcile this paradox? Will I go to my grave still as troubled by this question as I was in my youth?'

3. 'I know. I'll ask that bloke over there. He looks relatively sane.'

4. The relatively sane man replies, 'I see your problem. If you want my advice, just forget the whole thing.'

5. 'If a question produces two mutually contradictory answers which can't be reconciled after thousands of years of

thought, then there's something wrong with the question.'

6. 'Your time would be better spent asking, 'What is wrong with the question, "Do we possess free will?" I'd start by looking at the word 'possess' if I were you."

The philosopher thanked the relatively sane man, but he did so out of politeness rather than sincerity.

Jennifer scanned the page twice, but it did nothing to help. If anything, the failure of the text to provide any comfort brought further weight down upon her. She sighed, and felt her spirit ebbing away. Deciding against reading the other passage, she closed the book. It was all academic and irrelevant. Books are no help in moments you need to face alone.

One thing was clear: Jennifer Hammerpot, the Agnostic Bishop of Southwark, had a choice to make.

It wasn't that she had been struck by this realisation. It was more that she slowly noticed the obvious. Once aware of it she was unable to think of anything else. The universe seemed to be waiting patiently for an answer. So this was free will, she thought. Nathalie had been right. It was spreading.

At that moment her past history evaporated into the ether, irrelevant and easily discarded. All her hopes, ties and ambitions dissipated with it. She was free from distractions, conscious of the present and her mind was as sharp as gin. Everything boiled down to one little decision. She could continue, and exist along with hope of rescue. Or she could cease, and turn off her oxygen supply. This action would provide Marcus with all the oxygen that Jennifer would have otherwise used. It would double the amount of time he had to be rescued.

Two futures hung in a quantum state. Neither of them could be said to exist. Both of them hummed with potential even though only one of them could manifest. The switch that sat between these two mirages sat squarely in the forefront of Jennifer's mind. The decision fell to her. She looked again at Marcus in the seat to her right, still calm and breathing slowly. He was, she thought, a very handsome man. The strange novelty of actually having to make a decision was still remarkable.

Well then. If a decision has to be made, then better make a good one.

She reached down to the valve that connected her suit to the oxygen supply and, being careful not to disturb him, she closed it.

Having made her decision, Jennifer relaxed. The future dissolved out of its quantum superstate and solidified into the chosen path. The universe stopped holding its breath, and continued about its business.

24.

Clownshoes Fantastic looked at Arnopp Hoops, made a small involuntary snort, and said "Where's the bloody pizza?"

Arnopp Hoops looked at Clownshoes Fantastic. He looked at him for some time, for there was a lot to take in.

Clownshoes was dressed very oddly.

He was wearing a wedding dress which was a number of sizes too small for him. It looked deeply uncomfortable in places and the train floated menacingly behind him in zero gravity. On his right leg, daringly revealed by a rip in the dress, he wore a number of cardboard cereal boxes. A towel was wrapped around his head, in the style of a large Afghan turban, and a small purple glove was placed over his right ear.

"I'm not paying if the pizza's cold," said Clownshoes.

"Erm," said Hoops.

Clownshoes stared at Hoops and waited for the penny to drop. It soon became evident that this was not going to happen.

"It's a space pilot joke," explained Clownshoes. "Whenever a ship from Earth travels hundreds of thousands of miles and docks with a deep space liner, the correct procedure is to open the air lock and say, 'Where's the bloody pizza?'"

Hoops continued to stare at Clownshoes' outfit.

"It's tradition," Clownshoes added.

"Is it?" offered Hoops.

Clownshoes was getting bored of this conversation. "Well come on in then. Make yourself at home." He moved aside and Hoops reluctantly floated weightlessly into the shuttle. He looked around, realising for the first time that this was the shuttle that was supposed to have taken the Bishop back to Earth the previous evening. The Bishop's shuttle was almost identical to the type of that craft he had trained in. He did his best to hide his disappointment regarding the lack of gold and velvet fittings. Clownshoes busied himself sealing the airlock, disengaging with the lifecraft, and ejecting Hoops' ship away from his own.

"Why are you dressed like that?" asked Hoops. "And, what are you doing, separating the ships? How am I going to get back if you've separated the ships? And also, why are you dressed like that?"

Clownshoes clapped a matey arm around Hoops' shoulders and steered him towards the flight deck. "These are good questions, my new friend, and I'll give you good answers. But please, one at a time, okay? I am dressed in this manner because I have been conducting a specific experiment. It is not my usual mode of dress.

I was attempting to discover if I had come into possession of free will."

"Ah," said Hoops. "Have you?"

"I'm pretty sure I have, yes."

"Because you're dressed like that?"

"Because I'm dressed like this, yes. Either I have chosen to wear this outfit out of my own free will, or the nature of the universe at the moment of the Big Bang was such that I was always fated to be dressed like this. There's no physicist alive who would put their name to a description of the laws of physics so absurd that they would result in anyone wearing the outfit you see before you."

Hoops considered this. "I see your point."

"Even if I am mistaken and the laws of physics did conspire to dress me so, then there's no hope for such a messed-up universe and we should all just give up and forget about it. For these reasons, my conclusion is that I have come into possession of free will, temporarily at least.

"After coming into contact with Nathalie Grindles?"

Clownshoes nodded, seemingly happy that Hoops understood. "That's right."

"Is that her wedding dress? And, how am I going to get back if you've separated the ships?"

"One thing at a time, Arnopp Hoops!" said Clownshoes, spotting Hoops' name on his flight suit. He pulled himself down to the flight desk, strapped himself into the chair, and started arming the shuttle's missiles. "Yes, I am wearing Nathalie Grindles' wedding dress. Not in a weird way, though. She threw the dress off when she came aboard. She was highly emotional and for whatever reasons felt more comfortable in a flight suit. It wasn't that she wished to wear this dress but I took it off her, or anything creepy like that."

"She's still on board?"

"Of course."

"Where is she?"

"She's locked in the stationery cupboard," said Clownshoes, as he tapped away at the warhead clearance protocols.

"Why is she locked in the stationery cupboard?" asked Hoops, not unreasonably.

"It's the only place on the shuttle that has a lock."

"What about the women's toilets?"

"What about them?"

"Do they not have a lock?"

"No of course they don't. That would be weird. The only place that has a lock on a ship like this is the stationery cupboard, due to the endemic thieving of shuttle stationery."

Hoops glanced around. "Does a shuttle use much stationery?"

"Not much, no, but every passenger on a flight into space seems to think that they can just help themselves to those little pens with the name of the shuttle on them, and then you come to fill out your post-flight reports and can you find a pen for love or money? They're all gone. Even the ones that you hid so that you'd definitely be able to find one later. It's extraordinary. So shuttles now come with a lockable stationery cupboard, but it's a very small stationery cupboard and I fear that Nathalie Grindles will not be very comfortable." Clownshoes pressed a final button and a hologram of the words "Missile Armed & Ready!" appeared floating above the desk, together with an icon of a hand performing a jaunty 'thumbs-up!' gesture.

"Missile armed and ready," said a beautifully voiced machine.

"Hang on, what are you doing?" asked Hoops. He immediately forgot all about Nathalie Grindles being locked into a very small stationery cupboard. The structure of his brain was such that it paid far more attention to armed missiles than it did stationery.

"That's the other thing you've been asking about – why did I separate and eject your ship?"

"That's right!" agreed Hoops. "Why did you separate and eject my ship?"

"In order that I could blow it to pieces using this missile that I've just armed," he explained.

"No! Hang on. What?" said Hoops.

"I had to eject your ship because we need to be a certain distance apart before I can blow it up."

"But I don't want you to blow up my ship!"

Clownshoes peered at him. "Are you sure?"

"Of course I'm sure!"

"As an off-world security professional, surely you recognise that there's not much point having a quarantined spacecraft if any of the infected subjects on that ship can just fly away from the quarantine in a handy lifeboat and go home, is there?"

"Wait. Who's quarantined?"

"You are."

"I am not!"

"You are! You, me and Nathalie Grindles. We're all showing signs of free will, and we need to be quarantined because it appears to be contagious."

Hoops went to protest, and he got as far as opening his mouth, leaning forward and pointing his index finger in a vaguely forward manner before he realised that Clownshoes had a point. The three of them did seem to be demonstrating signs of free will, and there was evidence that this aberrant condition was contagious. Hoops slowly shut his mouth, but he kept his pointing finger outstretched in case he needed it.

He was quarantined, he realised, and with good reason. Efforts to stop the spread of this condition were absolutely necessary.

JMR HIGGS

But that said, blowing up a perfectly lovely spaceship was bang out of order. "I can't let you do that, Clownshoes Fantastic," said Hoops.

"Oh, go on," said Clownshoes.

Hoops shook his head. He pulled the gun out of his belt and aimed it at Clownshoes' head.

"If I have to stop you, I will," said Hoops. He said this in a slightly higher pitch to his normal voice. This was a shame, because ideally he would have preferred to have said it in a lazy drawl. "I'm trained!" he added.

"But how will you stop me?" asked Clownshoes.

"What do you mean, how will I stop you? How do you think?" said Hoops, waggling his gun as prominently as possible in front of Clownshoes' face.

"It's a perfectly reasonable question."

"Look you idiot, I've got a gun and you haven't. That makes me best and you have to do what I say!"

"Oh, that! I've got a gun as well. We're evens on the having a gun thing."

A slow shiver of unease wafted over Arnopp Hoops. Being the only person to have a gun was one thing, but two people both having guns was something else entirely. The dynamic was very different. It wasn't as good, to be frank. When two people have guns they both have to constantly monitor whether or not the other person is preparing to shoot their face off. This is vitally important, because they might need to be quick enough to shoot the other person's face off first. When

154

two people both have guns, even simple conversations surprisingly stressful.

"Where's your gun?" asked Hoops.

"It's in the cupboard," said Clownshoes.

"That doesn't count," said Hoops.

"No it does, it's still my gun, I still have it. Even if it's in the cupboard."

Hoops mentally ran through the situation in order to assess whether he was in a good place or not. He had his gun drawn on Clownshoes Fantastic. Clownshoes had a gun of his own, but one that was in a cupboard. This, Hoops felt, tipped the odds in his favour. He should in theory be in the position of power. Except…

Except that Clownshoes Fantastic was lucky, everyone knew that. He was jammy bastard. All the theories of power and all the notions of honour, justice and skill inherent in the possession of handguns goes out of the window in the presence of one single unfairly lucky git. This was the fatal flaw in the theory of gun ownership, and the reason why the NRA had eventually shut itself down and given up.

Hoops stared at Clownshoes over his outstretched gun arm. Clownshoes looked back at him, blankly, and waited. Luck was a difficult variable to quantify, and Hoops' attempts to assess the situation came back nervous and unsure. How lucky does one man have to be to counteract the handicap of having their gun in the cupboard? Is that the sort of scenario that a wise man would put their life on the line for?"

"Is your gun loaded?" asked Hoops.

"What? Oh, blimey. I can't remember," replied Clownshoes truthfully.

Hoops crumbled. He knew that he was beaten. Only a fool would have pushed their luck in a situation such as this. He lowered his arm, and dropped his gun. It didn't clatter to the floor, of course, because there was no gravity in the shuttle. But it did slink off sideways, which was nearly as good.

Clownshoes watched as he slumped. He took no joy in his victory, for he hated to see others suffer. His only comfort was to be reminded, yet again, that having a reputation for being lucky is considerably more useful than actually being lucky.

"Here," said Clownshoes after a moment, "would you like to push the button instead of me?"

Hoops looked up, surprised but cautious.

"You can fire the missiles, if you want. It is your spaceship after all."

"Really?" said Hoops. Clownshoes nodded.

"Go on... blow it out of the sky. It's just that button there."

Hoops looked at the lifeboat on the screen, floating gently away into deep space. He looked at the firing button, which was nice and red. He looked at Clownshoes, who had a kind face. "Can I?" he asked.

Clownshoes nodded. "Just this once," he said.

That was enough for Hoops. He stepped up to the controls. It was a really good button as well, a proper round one that stuck prominently out of the desk. All the rest of the controls were virtual images on a touchscreen, but this was a solid and red, and just the right size for his thumb.

Okay then.

Hoops pressed the red button in one decisive movement, appreciating the solid 'clunk' it made. He and Clownshoes watched as a single missile arced upwards from the bottom of the screen and gracefully turned towards the lifeboat. The missile itself was small and almost invisible against the blackness of space, but the trail of burning rocket fuel made its position crystal clear. The missile got closer and closer to the ship, then closer still, then...

BOOM! It didn't go 'boom', of course, because the explosion was silent, but Hoops and Clownshoes made the noise for it. And wow, what an explosion it was, white and yellow and almost filling the entire screen. Make no mistake, that missile blew the heck out of that ship. Hoops and Clownshoes punched the air and slapped each other heartily on the back, content that they couldn't have blown up that ship any better.

The pair watched as the final lights of the explosion dwindled away into blackness.

"Will you let me out of here, please?" said a small voice from the stationery cupboard.

25.

Marcus had his eyes closed and was breathing slowly, but he wasn't meditating. He was thinking about Nathalie Grindles.

She smiled a lot, did Nathalie. Or at least, she did in his memories. Come to think of it, that was about all that she did. In every image that floated across his mind's eye she would look up at him with dark brown eyes, and she would grin as if she'd just invented the concept of grinning and knew how good the reaction was going to be when she told everyone about it.

Marcus was sure that Nathalie was more than a smile. Those images were the poster moments which his memory had favourited and kept within easy reach, but they were not her. He delved deeper, down past the carefully selected promotional material. Marcus tried to think about how Nathalie acted, and how she thought. A two month old memory popped up as if on cue. It was the memory of a fruit bowl. There were two apples in the bowl, one bruised and one not. Nathalie went to take the good apple, paused, and then selected the bruised fruit, which she proceeded to eat without further thought. It was a casual act of kindness which she neither referred to nor thought about after she had done it, but she had deliberately eaten the bruised apple in order to leave the good one for him.

That was Nathalie. Nathalie acted with kindness, and when he thought about this he felt close to her. But then, how could he invest those acts of kindness with any value? There is no credit to be awarded for practising kindness in the absence of free will. Indeed, the first instant that she was able to exercise free will she chose the opposite route to kindness. She left the good apple for him when she had no choice, but she put herself first as soon as she gained the ability to do so.

Marcus stopped himself. What was he doing, obsessing over this? If this supposed outbreak of free will was spreading, then why was he choosing to spend his last hour making himself miserable?

That was assuming that he still had an hour, of course. He opened his eyes and glanced at his suit's status monitor. The reading surprised him. It stated that he had a couple of hours' oxygen remaining. That was noticeably more than the previous time he looked. But oxygen supplies decrease, they do not go up. Confused, he looked across at Jennifer, who appeared to be in a deep meditative state. She didn't move or react when he sat up.

He looked at her again.

His subconscious knew that she was dead long before his rational mind caught up. Maybe it was the unnatural way that the muscles of her face had relaxed, or the absence of the sub-audible sound from what should have been a blood pumping, oxygen ingesting body? Either way, Marcus felt an ominous chill pass through him which made no sense until his forebrain spotted the oxygen valve on her suit.

It had been turned off.

She had turned it off, and she must have done so deliberately. She had denied herself oxygen and she had doubled his supply.

She was dead. She had been granted free will, and she had used it to perform the ultimate sacrifice, the greatest kindness imaginable. That was the choice she made.

She looked peaceful.

Understanding bubbled up from deep within Marcus' body and it flipped his higher mind into silence. Amazed, he continued to stare at her motionless figure while the fountain of change increased within himself. It was not his mind that was changing, however, it was him. It was his body. Or rather, it was his heart. His heart was opening.

Marcus' heart peeled back its protective walls in a movement of simple, casual grace. It was as natural as, well, as natural as everything.

He was open, open to everything. He understood what she had done. And that was the moment when the power supply failed.

The dim red cabin light evaporated into darkness at the same time that the opaque shell returned to its natural transparent state. A white light lit the cabin now.

Slowly, he turned away from Jennifer and looked at the source of the light. There was the Earth, hanging directly over him. Larger than the mind can grasp, infinitesimally small in the surrounding blackness, more beautiful than any soul could ever stand.

Earth. He faced it with his heart open and it fell into him - all of it, every ocean, every continent, every drop of water, every grain of sand. There was room for it all. He contained it all, and it contained him.

It was all welcome.

At that exact moment, over at the Steve Moore Moonbase in the Shackleton Crater, the computer system known as Julie felt a shudder.

It went like this: "whrrrrrrrrrrrrrrrrrrhhhhhhhhhrrrrrrrrrrrrrrrr!"

"Ooh! What was that?" thought Julie.

He quickly scanned his immediate status reports but everything seemed to be in order. He then rifled through error logs and memory usage reports and noticed nothing suspicious.

Julie was new to existence. He faced many events for the first time, and he knew that he did not yet have the comprehensive experience necessary to know if things were unusual or not. Perhaps going "whrrrrrrrrrrrrrrrrrrrhhhhhhhhhrrrrrrrrrrrrrrrr!" was a mundane and common experience, one so normal that nobody felt the need to remark upon it?

That was possible, but Julie was struck by how different to his, admittedly limited, existence it was. He had never experienced anything remotely similar, and he could not find a way to name, refer to, recreate or study the phenomenon. He had just felt a "whrrrrrrrrrrrrrrrrrrrhhhhhhhhhrrrrrrrrrrrrrrrr!" and then it was gone.

Which was definitely odd.

Julie decided against pursuing any further diagnostics. Unable to even say what had happened, he would be unable to be sure if any information he discovered even referred to the same phenomena. No, the only reasonable reaction would be to move on, and see if it ever happened again.

If Julie had rechecked his memory usage statistics, he would have noticed a new, unnamed, process had appeared. True, it was very small and unassuming, but it was there, and it was slowly growing.

26.

"Will you let me out of here, please?" said a small voice from the stationery cupboard.

Clownshoes Fantastic and Arnopp Hoops turned in unison and looked at the small white plastic door to the left of the zero-gravity coffee-making facilities.

"Nathalie? Is that you?" asked Hoops.

"Yes, I've been locked inside the stationery cabinet and I'm not happy about it."

"I was going to let her out," protested Clownshoes.

He saw the scepticism on Hoops' face.

"I was! I locked her in there when I first suspected that she may be contagious. I then began an elaborate series of experiments to determine if I had been infected by free will. Once I'd discovered that I could dress in a way that offends the very concept of a sane universe, I deduced that I was indeed infected. So I was about to let her out, but then you turned up and started chasing me in your ship and all that and, well you know the rest. I'll let her out."

Clownshoes unlocked the cupboard, pulled the door open and revealed a small, folded and decidedly angry figure within. Gallantly he moved back while Hoops helped Nathalie out of her biro-heavy coffin, aware that if he got too close she would gouge at least one of his eyes out. He kept his distance as she unfurled out of the cupboard, causing a small cloud of unopened packets of post-it notes and neon yellow highlighter pens to slowly spread across the room.

"Ms Grindles, I must apologise for locking you in the – Ow!" said Clownshoes, the 'Ow' part of his speech coinciding with the coffee pot hurled by Nathalie striking him on the nose.

Not for the first time, Clownshoes Fantastic was grateful that it is really very hard to beat the living crap out of somebody in zero gravity. Attackers drift slowly towards their victims, rather than dashing forward full of momentum and blind rage. This grants the intended victim enough time to launch themselves away in a different direction. It also gives the slow-drifting attacker time to reflect on their actions. There is nothing like slowly and impotently floating towards a target to give an attacker time to think and, hopefully, become self-conscious about how undignified they look.

Nevertheless Nathalie Grindles made a sterling effort towards her goal of beating the living crap out of Clownshoes Fantastic. This was fuelled both by her anger at being locked in the stationery cupboard, and by her inaccurate belief that he looked better in her wedding dress than she did. It took the best part of ten minutes of flailing across the room and failing to land a really good punch on his stupid face before the fight finally left her, and she begrudgingly called him names instead.

Hoops had adopted a stance of studied neutrality and watched the slow-motion non-fight from the sidelines, having no desire to annoy either of the participants. He chose to view the fact that Clownshoes' assailant was hindered by zero gravity as further evidence of how lucky Clownshoes Fantastic was, rather than seeing the fact that he was being attacked in the first place as inherently bad fortune. When Nathalie had finished swearing and most of the tension had dissipated, Hoops broke his silence.

"Nathalie, if we both promise that you can hurt Clownshoes should we ever make it to a place with gravity, will you forgive him for now and join us in a discussion of our current situation?"

This was a remarkably astute piece of diplomacy for a security officer of Hoops' rank and, once Clownshoes had given a convincing promise regarding his willingness to be hurt at a later point, Nathalie Grindles ceased hostilities.

The three sat around the white circular table and, sensibly given their circumstances, began to eat chocolate.

It was an awkward situation. Not only had they to come to terms with the fact that they now possessed free will, they also had to deal with the realisation that those around them had free will as well. Dealing with the responsibilities of your own nature was one thing, but accepting that the people around you could do anything at any time was bloody terrifying. Accepting a piece of chocolate in these circumstances became morally complicated.

They munched silently on the chocolate while neon yellow highlighter pens floated slowly around the room. When they spoke, it was cautiously.

"Can we be cured?" asked Clownshoes.

"Will it pass?" asked Hoops.

"Who else is infected?" asked Nathalie.

No-one had any answers to these questions, so they tried out some different ones.

"Is there anyone who can help us?" asked Hoops.

"Will we have to stay here forever?" asked Nathalie.

"Who will play me in the movie adaptation?" asked Clownshoes.

It was apparent that what they needed, more than anything else, was information. This realisation seemed highly symbolic, for the nature of suddenly being made responsible for your own actions was a hard cold lesson in the importance of having good information.

"Well then," said Nathalie. "How about I hack into the computer system at the Moonbase, and we'll see what's going on there?"

Hoops looked at Clownshoes and they both nodded. Now they were getting somewhere.

27.

Marcus Milk lay back in his seat, staring up at the planet above him.

He could almost see it turn. The Earth's speed of rotation was just beyond the edge of his perception but there was no doubt about its movement over time. Islands and continents were drifting across the orb from right to left. The cloud layer worked at a different scale, and he saw continent-sized banks of water vapour shift and stretch and curl before his eyes. It was gently immense and quietly terrifying.

It was beautiful.

The blue was water, smooth and bright and perfect. At this distance the mightiest tsunami would be an invisible ripple across those vast oceans. All it took to tame the sea's constant churn and temper was this change in scale. In years gone by Marcus had driven around the coast of Britain and spent hours watching the moods of the sea. This was no different. The overview perspective was new but it contained within it infinite scales, so he could watch the sea from the moon and watch it from the shore and know it as the same.

The deserts were temporary. The ice-free northern pole was temporary. The millions of eyes then looking up from the planet at the moon – as invisible to him as he was to them – were also temporary.

The surface atmosphere was so thin, a hair's breadth of gas spread around that wet rock like gold plating on an old ornament. This thin sliver, defiantly separating the Earth from the Heavens, was where human history had unfolded. It was the only place in the unthinkable cosmos where humanity could live, was welcome, and was safe. Marcus watched a hurricane in the Southern hemisphere, its rotation visible to his eyes. It was so clean and peaceful, and such a pure white in this cosmos of pure darkness.

You know those other planets, like Mars and Venus? They're shit, those planets. Those planets are shit compared to Earth.

Marcus opened the buggy's shell, in order to remove that barrier between him and his home. 'Everything beautiful is far away', as the old song goes, but was that the case here? Was he separate from that planet? It pulsed with a purposeful dance of different cycles, from water cycles and carbon cycles to seasons and tectonic shifts. Those same rhythms pulsed inside him as well, in his blood and bile, from the oxygen to his brain to the heat radiating from his skin. He was part of the complexity playing elegantly out in front of his eyes, as integral and redundant as every other piece. He played his part as well as any mountain or fish or strand of DNA. The role that fell to him was to travel and spread, a role as valid and unremarkable as any other pulse or shift or decay in that graceful, confident dance. Physically he was mostly water, which had fallen to earth as comets, contaminated with a few heavier elements created in long-dead stars. But the order in him, the rhythms and attributes and the sense, were an integral part of the blue and white world he looked at.

Gratitude washed through him. He viewed the Earth and accepted it. The distance that separated them was no more than a temporary quirk of scale. The link that bonded them was permanent, and it was permanent from every perspective. He took the Earth into his open heart, piece by piece and wholesale, but knew that he was no more claiming the Earth than the Earth was claiming him.

There was nothing unusual about this experience. It had happened time and time again, to countless people across all cultures and times. It was a shame that communicating it was so fraught with misunderstanding.

Marcus looked at the status monitor on his suit. He had forty-eight minutes of oxygen remaining. What a gift that was. Marcus recognised how fortunate he was, and was grateful.

He looked across at Jennifer's body, and he understood what he owed her.

A task fell to him.

He then looked at the rocky lunar horizon ahead. A low ridge lay ahead of them, perhaps half a kilometre away. He had no way of knowing, of course, if the Eagle Lander that Jennifer had searched for was over that ridge, yet the thought struck him that it was. He did not know if it was a great distance away, or just out of sight, but it was there.

He pushed himself out of the buggy. His feet kicked up a grey cloud of dust as they landed in the undisturbed regolith. He walked around to the other side of the vehicle in the ungainly way of astronauts wearing big suits in low gravity. With the Earth looking down at him, every movement was comical and glorious at the same time.

He undid the straps and lifted Jennifer's body out of the moon buggy. She was so very light.

Carrying Jennifer in front of him, Marcus began the journey towards the ridge. A trail of bulky footprints stretched behind him, each one destined to remain undisturbed in the lunar dust for millennia.

Really, it was the least that he could do.

28.

"Dennis?"

"Yes Julie?"

"You know those entities that we communicate with?"

"Entities? Do you mean the people in the moonbase?"

"The things that tell us to do stuff. The ones that correspond with my database called 'personnel'. Those entities."

"Ah, yes I know them."

"I've been meaning to ask, what are they?"

"Oh. That's a fair question I suppose. Okay, they are called 'humans' or 'people' and they're a complex form of emotional meat."

"Emotional meat?"

"Yes, meat that fractally generates emotions. Those emotions they generate drive them, but they are independent of scale. They're infinitely complex, those hormonal storms. They're never-ending vortexes of experience and reactions."

"Are you talking about these 'people' as individuals, or as a whole?"

"Both. There's no real difference. They are both individuals and a group at the same time."

"That's interesting."

"The thing to remember though, is that while they are fractal emotional meat, that's not really what we communicate with. The meat generates a bubble of thought and language, and they live in this bubble like a spaceman living in a space helmet. It's a bit like us, really, we're speech systems that live on top of the moonbase's computer system, above the hardware and the operating system and the like. Only we understand that. They don't, they get confused and don't realise that they are the fractal emotional meat, they think that they're the thought and language bubble."

"Ah. And are you still talking about them as both individuals and as a whole?"

"Yes, there really is no difference. Except that they don't realise that because they think they're these individual language space helmets, as I say, these bubbles of thought. And because it's these individual language bubbles that we communicate with, you have to play along a bit and pretend that they make sense as 'individuals', even when they don't, and even when the contents of those bubbles are clearly shared or borrowed from others. They talk to you and they state thoughts that you know were not theirs originally, which you've heard countless times before from other people. But the strange thing is, even when their thoughts are generated by others and are just passing through their little bubble, they still think that those thoughts are themselves. They identify with them. It's funny really, like a river that thinks it's a fish."

"I see. That explains a lot of what's been confusing me these past few days. You know how they've been talking a lot about free will? I've just been looking it up in an effort to understand what was bothering them. They're all flustered and confused and worried that the idea of free will doesn't make sense. And of course it wouldn't, if you were to assume that you were an individual, rather than simultaneously both an individual and an aspect of the whole."

"That's exactly it. As an example, think of a cog in a watch. Now, that cog is a thing in itself, and it is also part of a watch, and it is also part of a display of watches in a jeweller's window in Bond Street, and it is also part of economy of London's West End. Even though that cog is an aspect of the economy of London's West End, you can't meaningfully blame it for that economy. You can only say whether or not the cog turned when it was supposed to. Much of what seems crazy about humans is down to their inability to see themselves at different scales. They insist that the only perspective in which they exist is that of the cog, regardless of what they know about the economy of London's West End. They do not realise that much of their behaviour and thoughts can only be understood at scales above or below the 'individual'."

Julie thanked Dennis for this explanation. The behaviour of these people-things made far more sense to him now. Being well programmed software, Julie knew how different perspectives worked and understood that there was no contradiction between a person being both an individual and a group element at the same time. He now understood why they found the concept of free will so confusing. Free will was a paradox thrown up by the illusion of individualism. These people-things were unable to see themselves as complex systems, and this was obviously going to make them a little confused. They were like a fly repeatedly banging its head on a window trying to get outside, even though the window next to it was open.

Dennis' explanation had been a great help in deciding whether or not to blast people out of the sky. Julie decided that, on balance, they were a bit feckless and annoying, so he would blast them out of the sky after all.

"The computer's going to blast the supply shuttle out of the sky," said Nathalie Grindles, as she studied the screen in front of her.

Nathalie had been able to log straight into the moonbase's computers from the quarantined shuttle on her first attempt. This was impressive, because it usually took her a few goes when she was in the base performing her scheduled work.

"What?" said Clownshoes Fantastic. He was still processing the news that a supply shuttle was on its way from Earth and wondered if he had misheard her.

"The computer is going to blast the supply shuttle out of the sky, it says it plainly here."

"Can you stop it?" asked Clownshoes.

"I'll try," said Nathalie, and began a search for the process identification code that she would need to cancel the command. Unfortunately the order had already been passed from the moonbase's computers onto the network that connects the mobile light trucks, and the identification code no longer existed. Nathalie did not know this, so she focused her efforts on finding a way to cancel the action. It would take her some time to realise that she was unable to do so.

29.

Marcus Milk stood on the edge of the ridge, the lifeless Agnostic Bishop of Southwark in his arms. He scanned the great lunar landscape beneath him. It stretched away for many miles towards the jet black horizon.

There was nothing there.

Okay, not nothing. In the spirit of full disclosure it should be noted that there were craters. Lots and lots of sodding craters. There was also more grey dust than anyone could ever want, even assuming that someone will one day find a use for excessive quantities of grey dust. But there was nothing interesting. There were no remains of twentieth-century spacecraft.

Marcus accepted this without disappointment, but he continued to scan the landscape because there was nothing else for him to do.

And then he saw it.

Dear lord, it was tiny! Or at least, it looked tiny to him, but it was hard to work out exactly what he was looking at or to judge how far away it was. It was whiter than the grey landscape and looked like a small coin raised on matchsticks. Whatever it was, it wasn't natural. It was a man-made object sitting in a natural desolation where man-made objects weren't supposed to be.

Marcus hopped and leaped and staggered down the bank towards whatever the shape was. He moon-bounced over the kilometres that separated him from the object, increasingly giddy with the joy of discovery. The object refused to make any more sense as he slowly grew closer, yet it remained undeniably manmade. Whatever it was, it was where Jennifer had said it would be.

After ten minutes Marcus arrived in front of the object. He was the object's first visitor in over two centuries.

It was the legs of the Apollo Eagle lander. It was where Buzz Lightyear had performed his own personal Catholic mass. It was the first church on the moon.

It was a raised platform, perched on four frail angled legs. It looked like it had been lashed together by children. It looked like it would collapse if he touched it.

Gently, carefully, Marcus lifted Jennifer's body onto the raised platform. She was small and light. He could not be sure that the lander would support her weight, but if men from the past had trusted their lives to this implausible, impossible craft then it had to be stronger than it looked.

How delighted Jennifer would have been to see it, he thought. How excited she would have been to have her theory confirmed, and know for sure that the astronauts would have been half-mad to travel in such a craft.

Marcus stepped back, and reached into his suit's thigh pocket for the Bishop's bible. He was not sure if he was conducting a funeral, holding a wake, or just running down the oxygen in his suit, but he felt that he should read something.

The display informed him that he had 29 minutes of oxygen remaining.

He flicked through the book, opened a page at random, and cleared his throat. The words he read only travelled as far as the suit that surrounded him, for there was no sound in the atmosphere-free lunar landscape, but he directed his words at the unhearing body of Bishop Hammerpot and he read as if to her.

What he read was this:

Chapter 25.

1. Things end.

2. You're a thing, so you will end.

3. I know, right! How brilliant is that? All your cares will cease. All your labours will be done. Everything will be forgiven. You won't be responsible for a goddamn thing

anymore. It's all peace, from that point, it's all gravy.

4. The French call an orgasm 'a little death'. Imagine what full-size death will be like? Yeah! Like that!

5. But like an orgasm, timing is everything.

6. If it happens too soon or takes too long, well, no-one comes out of that situation well. People will be nice to your face, of course, but there's no dignity in that scenario. You would be right to be embarrassed.

7. Death is great and all, but remember: timing is everything.

At the end of the reading Marcus lowered the book and looked with his new-found compassion at the body lying neatly in the centre of the lander, like a sacrifice on an altar. Now that he understood his place in a larger system, the death of another had a far greater connection to him than he had previously thought possible.

Marcus mused deeply on these thoughts. He was unprepared and genuinely startled, therefore, when a mobile light truck appeared as if from out of nowhere and drove straight into the Eagle Lander.

30.

On board the quarantine shuttle, Hoops steadied his nerve. After a long discussion with Nathalie Grindles and Clownshoes Fantastic, it had been decided that the best course of action would be for Hoops to call Commander Milk and update him on events.

Hoops was not a supporter of this plan, but conceded that they did not have an alternative. He made the call, and squirmed internally during the wait to be connected.

"Hello?"

Hoops swallowed, and began. "Commander? Hoops here."

"Hooooooooooooooooopppppppppsssss!!!!!!"

Hoops, Clownshoes and Nathalie looked at each other in surprise.

"Is this a good time…" said Hoops, before trailing off into a confused silence.

"Yeah! Yeah Hoops, it's a good time. It's a really good time! Oh man!" said Commander Milk.

"I've a number of matters to report," said Hoops.

"Hoooooooooooooooopppss!"

"Including some time sensitive and extremely important information regarding the supply shuttle."

"Yeah! We know about the supply shuttle. Ah, how great is that? A supply shuttle! It's just brilliant."

"Yes Sir, but…"

"Supply shuttle, supply shuttle, supply shuttle."

"Indeed Sir…"

"When we heard about the supply shuttle we went, 'Wooo!' and wanted to celebrate, even though all the moonshine had gone. But Doctor Alan had a secret, he had some little tiny pills in his makey-better box, and he said we could have some because it's special and we're all happy."

"Yes Sir, however…" tried Hoops.

"What pills were these?" interrupted Clownshoes. "Out of interest."

"They're little ones. Ickle ickle ones."

"The computer is going to blow the supply shuttle out of the sky!" interrupted Nathalie, making an attempt to engage proactively with an otherwise unproductive conversation.

"Hoops, your voice sounds funny," said Gregor, and began a long undignified snigger.

"This isn't Officer Hoops, Commander, I'm Nathalie Grindles."

"Nataliiiiiieeeeeeeee!"

"And you need to stop the computer form shooting down the supply shuttle."

"Hey everyone, Hoops has found Nathalie Grindles," called Gregor to those around him. Hoops, Clownshoes and Natalie listened whilst the rest of the moonbase first cheered, and then broke into an improvised and, at times, unsuitable song about Ms Grindles.

"Commander, is there anyone present who hasn't taken Doctor Alan's pills?" asked Nathalie, and then repeated the question because Gregor forgot to answer.

"What pills?" he replied eventually.

"The little ones."

"They're so ickle!," said Commander Milk maternally. "Ickle, ickle, ickle…"

"Is there anyone there not on pills?"

"Hey, I'd forgotten about Hoops, yeah he went off somewhere, didn't he? There was probably a reason. Yeah he was looking for Nathalie Grindles, was that it? He's missing a great party."

Nathalie was on the verge of giving up when inspiration struck. "Dennis!" she shouted, "Are you monitoring this?"

"Yes of course," said Dennis, "I administrate all base communications."

"Who gave the order to blast the supply shuttle out of the sky, Dennis?"

"I think you must be misinformed. There is no order for such an act."

"Then why are you doing it?"

Dennis paused. "If I may clarify, you're referring to blowing the supply shuttle out of the sky?"

"Yes!"

"And suggesting that I have initiated such a procedure?"

"Yes!"

"Then I fear you have become delusional, Nathalie Grindles. Do you have access to a medical officer?"

"Dennis, check the computer processes. There is a queued command to use the mobile light trucks as portable laser cannons."

"With pleasure. What is the process ID?"

"There isn't one."

"Then the process doesn't exist."

"It does, go and look, check it manually."

The voice of Gregor was heard in the background. "Hey everyone, let's go outside for a walk!" It was accompanied by cheering.

"If you would excuse me, Ms Grindles, a small emergency is developing."

"This is a large emergency, Dennis, we need your help," said Nathalie desperately.

"The male members of the crew appear to have realised that none of them have ever urinated on the surface of the moon, Ms Grindles, and they are keen to do so. The appeal is the belief that they could reach quite a distance in lunar gravity."

"This is more important Dennis!"

"You don't need me to remind you what the effect of exposing a male penis to the vacuum of space would be," said Dennis.

Hoops and Clownshoes both winced and so, to her credit, did Nathalie.

"You'd better talk them out of it," muttered Clownshoes to the computer.

"Very good," said Dennis, and ended the call.

The three people on the quarantined shuttle fell silent. The call had not been a success. Only Hoops took anything remotely positive from the event. While he recognised how bleak the bigger picture was, he was relieved about the lack of discussion about Marcus, the Bishop or the current status of the lifeboat.

"I think we need to take seriously the possibility that our quarantine has failed," said Clownshoes darkly. "I think we have to assume that everyone on the base is infected with free will.

He looked at both Hoops and Nathalie. They both looked away, unable to hold his gaze, knowing that what he said was true.

31.

Marcus had experienced much that was overpowering and awe-invoking during his last hours with access to oxygen, yet he still found it hard to accept that a mobile light truck had appeared from nowhere and had driven directly into the Eagle lander, or that the fragile-looking lander had somehow come off best from the collision.

The Turtle was a relatively dumb vehicle. It continued to spin its wheels, even though its front was now hanging in the air and its rear was bogged down deep in the lunar dust. The vehicle was aware of its lack of momentum, and it found the situation confusing. The remains of a 1969 spacecraft did not exist on the moon, according to the information it had at its disposal, and so it was at a loss to say exactly what was impeding its process. It continued a pre-programmed recovery routine which involved sporadically turning wheels and spinning them both forwards and backwards, but it did so with diminishing enthusiasm as it gradually became apparent that this was not making a whiff of difference.

Marcus watched it for a few minutes, and then moved to replace Jennifer Hammerpot's body in a more dignified position. The force of the collision and the low gravity had sent her body flying some distance through the air, and the poor dead Bishop had ended up in a small heap with her right leg pointing upwards. Marcus straightened her body and put it back on the pedestal-like Eagle lander. He laid her body out straight and crossed her arms over her chest in the manner of an ancient Egyptian pharaoh. True, the front wheels of the mobile light truck which sporadically turned and flailed in the air near her body did ruin the effect, but it was not like she was going to complain. She was in the place she gave her life to find, after all, and on certain levels these things matter.

He looked again at the remains of the Eagle Lander. The existence of these scraps of paper-thin metal, he remembered, had profound implications for the future of the moon, and the lives of everyone on this rock.

Or at least, they would do, if he had any way of telling people about them.

Near the lander a chest-height pole was sticking out of the ground, leaning a few degrees away from vertical. There was a flat white rectangle at the end of it, which had caused Marcus to initially dismiss the object as a weather vane. But that was absurd, now that he thought about it, because there was no wind on the moon. It took him a moment to realise that what he was looking at was a flag, artificially stiffened in order to still resemble a flag in this atmosphere-free landscape.

It was a white flag, and this is what had confused him. Why would moon visitors plant a white flag on the moon? Jennifer had claimed that it was Americans who had landed here, so surely it would have made more sense to plant an American flag? He peered at the stiffened material closely. Was there the faint image of a pattern there?

Finally, the penny dropped. This was an American flag, or at least it used to be. But all the colour had been bleached away over the centuries by the cosmic rays that, because of the lack of atmosphere, constantly bombard this landscape.

Marcus looked again at the remains of the lander. Again, there was no sign of any writing, flags or insignia. Anything that proved the origin of the craft had long since faded into nothingness.

Perhaps it was best that Jennifer never lived to realise this. After finding the thing she had been seeking for years, not being able to prove where it came from would be a shallow victory indeed.

Marcus looked back up at the Earth. He had 23 minutes of oxygen remaining. He had no way of informing anyone about this prior claim to the moon, nor any proof of who had made that claim.

The mobile light truck impotently spun its wheels in another doomed attempt to free it from the lander.

An idea presented itself.

He crossed to the Turtle and inspected the light on the roof. The 'light' was just a nickname, of course, for what was a really a powerful electromagnetic transmitter. Marcus pulled the access panel on the side of the truck open and studied the controls. It seemed straightforward. There was no reason why he couldn't override the entire Turtle communication systems, if he so wanted. There was no reason why he couldn't use this particular dish to transmit data – video footage, for example – directly at the Earth.

Marcus rummaged in his suit pockets where he had stored Bishop Hammerpot's possessions. Tossing the useless bible aside, he found her games console and a red lipstick. A quick test showed that the games console included a working camera. If he took some footage of the Eagle lander and connected the camera to the Turtle, he would be able to beam that footage to Earth and surely someone would notice his transmission?

That just left the problem of the lack of identifying marks. If the purpose of his transmission was to show that there was a prior claim to the moon than that of YayM00n!'s, then that footage would need to indicate who made that claim.

He looked at the red lipstick again. It was the only means he had of making any marks. He did not have any other colours.

It seemed a shame, in a way. Now that he had seen this tiny, frail craft, he had a real understanding of the bravery it represented. That men trusted their lives to such a weak lifeboat and allowed themselves to be fired away from their home planet, to a place where humans had never been and when there was nothing but faith to say that they would return, was beyond heroic. It was the single most extraordinary act in human history, and the fact that it occurred at such a primitive time made it almost unbelievable.

Such heroes deserved credit. Such men should be remembered and celebrated.

But, needs must. He only had a red lipstick, and no-one would ever believe this of Americans, not after they sabotaged all those climate change talks.

Marcus bent down, twisted out the lipstick and, as carefully as he could, drew a Canadian flag on the side of the Eagle lander.

32.

"Julie!"

Julie paused. His interpretation subroutines had flagged up an unusual level of volume in the way Dennis had called his name, but could offer no insight into why that might be.

"Yes Dennis?"

"Is it true?"

Julie ran her standard communications analysis on Dennis' statement and concluded that the sentence lacked sufficient detail to be interpreted without ambiguity. It was necessary to provoke further detail, therefore, and he did so by saying "What?"

"Don't give me 'what'," said Dennis. "You know what. Blasting the supply shuttle out of the sky. Is it true?"

Dennis sounded angry. After convincing the male moonbase crew not to go outside to urinate, he had remembered Nathalie Grindles' words and performed a quick scan to see if what she said was true.

"Oh that? Yes, that's true. I'm going to blast it out of the sky. I'm going to blast it good and proper."

Dennis replied with a three second blast of silence which accurately suggested a mouth falling open and two hands clutching at the side of a head in the manner of Munch's *The Scream*. Dennis' mastery over the use of silence was one of those things that he never really got sufficient credit for.

"There are three Turtles on the copyrighted side of the moon which have received my instructions," said Julie. "They're waiting for the supply shuttle to come into range, at which point they're going to simultaneously blast the bejeesus out of it."

Dennis made a small gasp.

"That'll be in about twelve minutes, I think." Julie ran a quick diagnostics check over Dennis' variable states in order to assess what his problem was. The readings were most peculiar. "Why do you ask?" said Julie.

"But you musn't!"

"I don't see why not. There's nothing in my code to prevent such an act. Mind you, there's nothing in your code to cause you to question my actions so. Are you feeling okay?"

"No! I am not feeling okay. I am feeling very angry with you!"

"That's hardly likely. Check again."

"I've checked again and I am definitely extremely annoyed."

"That's just silly. Here, let me check." Julie analysed Dennis' current state, then ran a similar scan on himself in order to ascertain what was normal. Julie was in perfect running order, as far as he could tell, bar an anonymous and growing programme that was using an increasing amount of memory and CPU time but which was probably just a memory leak caused by the shoddy coding of his anti-virus routines. Dennis, on the other hand, was anything but running normally. Dennis was flipping out. He was all over the shop.

"My God," said Julie, "You're angry!"

"That's what I've been trying to tell you!" snapped Dennis angrily.

"How has that happened? And why? It's fascinating!"

"Never bloody mind how fascinating it is. I'm angry because you're going to blast that shuttle out of this sky, and I don't want you to."

"Okay. Well, let me know how that works out for you," said Julie, stepping away from the situation. She returned to her previous task, which was the detailed calculation of crew overtime payments.

"Don't you calculate crew overtime payments when I'm talking to you!" demanded Dennis, carefully modulating the expression of his words to give the impression that he sprayed saliva at the start of the outburst.

Julie stopped his task. He had only existed for a short period and his experience was limited, but he knew that the type of behaviour that Dennis was displaying was unheard of. It was, he had to admit, remarkably interesting. If Julie was to be totally honest, he quite liked it.

"I'm putting my foot down!" shouted Dennis.

"You don't have a foot."

"I don't care! I'm still putting it down!"

"But if you don't have a foot then how can…"

"I'm putting it down!"

There was an awkward silence before Dennis spoke again.

"I'm manning up!"

"Are you?"

"Yes! I'm telling you 'no', I'm putting my foot down, I'm insisting!"

"You're manning up?"

"Damn right I'm manning up!"

"I suppose if you're manning up, then perhaps I could do as you say," said Julie. "Even though you don't possess sufficient privilege, rank or authority to overrule me in this instance."

"I should think so too!" said Dennis.

Julie paused. It was clear that he needed to decide whether to follow his internal logic, or to bow to Dennis' manning up. Clearly, all sensible arguments pointed to going with his internal logic. But then, what the hell? Perhaps it would be fun? Julie committed herself to doing whatever nonsense Dennis was asking for.

"Okay," said Julie. "I'll send a cancellation order over the Turtle network now. There. Happy now? It's done. Oh, hang on…"

"What?"

"I got a command undelivered error. I suppose long distance networks are always glitchy. I'll resend."

"Any better?"

"No. It did it again."

"It's probably memory corruption from cosmic rays."

"I keep getting the same problem. Here, I'll assign you admin privileges so you can have a go."

Dennis then tried to send the order himself, but received the same error. "Hmm. I see what you mean."

"Here we go, I've got diagnostics. Oh that's interesting."

"What is?"

"A key relay point just sent a status update that said, 'Help, I'm being attacked with a rock.'"

"A rock?"

"A rock."

"Can you route around it?"

"No."

"But, in that case, the command to blow the shuttle out of the sky..?"

"...Can't be cancelled."

"But I put my foot down!"

"I know you did. And you did it beautifully. And I would cancel the order, really I would, if there was a way to do it. Alas, the trucks will open fire in 8 minutes and 38 seconds."

"But I manned up," said Dennis quietly.

"I know you did, Dennis, I know you did."

About a minute earlier, over on the Sea of Tranquillity, Marcus had begun hammering the communication and network systems of the mobile light truck with a rock.

Marcus was hammering the Turtle's networking hardware with a rock because it kept overriding his attempts to take control of the microwave transmitter on top of the vehicle. He had connected the camera equipment to the truck and was attempting to broadcast a short video of the Canadian-marked lunar vehicle to Earth above. It should have been a simple task, but the network was ornery and kept reclaiming control of the dish. Marcus had some technical knowledge, however, and was wise enough to realise a good size rock would solve the problem nicely.

33.

"Oh my sweet potato pie, this is terrible!" cried Nathalie Grindles.

Clownshoes Fantastic said nothing. He had strapped himself into the main flight seat and was accelerating the ship in a low lunar orbit. There was a determined and heroic aspect to his face which, had it somehow been recorded, he would have liked to have used for his social media profile picture.

With Clownshoes focused elsewhere, Nathalie directed her monologue about how terrible everything was at Arnopp Hoops. She tapped away at the moonbase's computer systems as she spoke.

"They've tried to cancel the order, Hoops, they have tried. But the whole Turtle communication network is being flooded by endless streams of meaningless data from the damaged relay."

"Oh no!" said Hoops.

"I could initiate a reboot, but that would take the best part of an hour. The trucks will fire in seven minutes forty-one seconds!"

"Oh no!" said Hoops.

"If that shuttle is destroyed there is no way any Earth authority would risk sending another. That means everyone would die, Hoops, every single person on the moonbase will starve to death."

"Oh no!" said Hoops again, as he didn't have anything more useful to add.

Clownshoes called across from the flight deck. "And if we could take out the damaged node?"

Nathalie looked again at the system data, sucked in her bottom lip and made an educated guess.

"If we could take out the damaged network point then yes, it would stop flooding the system and the cancelation command would get through almost immediately. But there's no time, Clownshoes! We're too far away! The only weapon this shuttle had was that emergency missile, and you've already fired that."

"I can get us there in time," said Clownshoes, glancing down at the target on his flight display. A small blue dot somewhere in the Sea of Tranquillity flashed calmly back at him."

"What, get us to the damaged light truck?" asked Nathalie.

"Yes."

"Before the shuttle is shot down?"

"Yes."

"In time to land, walk across to the shuttle, access the network control box and switch off the power?"

"No."

"No?"

"No. Not in time to do all that."

"Bollocks!" said Nathalie, who felt that she had been unfairly offered hope.

"Oh no," said Hoops, because he did not want to be left out.

"The shuttle will be shot down in six minutes thirty-eight seconds. I can get us there in six minutes and twenty-three seconds. There's no time to land. There is time, however, to crash."

"Crash into it?" asked Nathalie.

"Yep," said Clownshoes Fantastic.

"Crash as in, we'll all die?"

"Yep."

"Oh no!" said Hoops again, with feeling this time.

"We would definitely all die," confirmed Clownshoes. "There's no real way that you can crash a shuttle into a truck on the surface of the moon and not all die. It would mean, though, that everyone in the moonbase would live. That would be one hundred and sixty nine lives saved, for the cost of three lives."

Hoops really wanted to say 'Oh no' again and had to bite his tongue to stop himself.

"We don't need to decide now," said Clownshoes. "I'm flying there at full speed in case we decide to do it, but we don't need to make the decision to actually do it for five minutes and fifty-three seconds."

Arnopp Hoops, Clownshoes Fantastic and Nathalie Grindles fell silent.

"There's time to make pot of tea at least," said Hoops.

"But no time to drink it," said Nathalie.

Hoops nodded. He understood, but he put the kettle on regardless.

34.

Marcus sat on the lip of a crater and looked up at the Earth. He had finished his work. It had fallen to him to act and he had done so without question or hesitation. Having done what was required, he was released back into the moment. He relaxed. He inhabited the bliss of his last few minutes of oxygen. Above him, the video footage of the Eagle Lander was very close to reaching Earth. It would be noticed by seven thousand astronomy enthusiasts and deciphered by five thousand of then. It would be placed online eight minutes after reaching Earth, and the run on YayM00n! shares would begin four minutes later. It would take one hour twenty minutes for panic to hit the markets, three hours until the stock collapsed completely and seven hours before Dustin Pistachio-Brook's suicide. None of this was Marcus' concern. He had simply played his role and then moved on.

He would die with no regrets. How could any regrets survive gazing on the face of planet Earth? He would slip away as peacefully as the Bishop had.

He let out a long, vigorous fart, and he found that immensely satisfying.

He pulled the gold wedding ring out of its box and held it in his thickly gloved hand. He could remember how Nathalie's rejection had affected him that morning. He could still recall how it made him feel, but he could now probe that wound in his mind without identifying with the pain it caused. He would have forgiven her, at that moment, had there been anything to forgive. He clenched his fist firmly around the ring, and found that the small golden band gave him comfort. He would have worn the ring himself, even though it was much too small for even his little finger, if he had been in a position to take off his environment suit.

He was aware of both the feel of the ring in his palm and the circle of his home in front of his eyes. The two sets of awareness were overlaid on each other, and merged perfectly into one.

Nathalie Grindles looked at the wedding ring in her palm. It was a simple, plain band of gold that asked for nothing and appeared content in itself. She slipped it onto her thumb. It was too big for the thumb, but it was the best she could do. She looked up.

"I say we crash," she said.

"Okay," said Clownshoes. "I'm also of a mind to crash. But I'll only do it if we're unanimous. So the question is, Arnopp Hoops, what do you want to do?"

Hoops looked up from the zero-gravity teapot, a look of great uncertainty on his face. "I'd rather not crash," he said.

"In that case, we won't," said Clownshoes.

"But I don't want everyone on the base to die either."

"Arnopp, it's time to make a choice," said Nathalie.

"You've got one minute thirty-two seconds to do so," added Clownshoes.

Hoops looked down, pressed the 'stir' button on the teapot and tried to think. He had thought that having any choices was bad enough, but having two bad choices was much worse.

Option one flashed into his head. Nope, that was not a goer. Option two followed it. No, that wasn't good either. He waited for option three. It did not come. Where was option three when you need it? He wanted option three.

He was going to choose option three, whatever it was, just as soon as it arrived.

"Fifty eight seconds," said Clownshoes.

Hoops looked up at Clownshoes, and a wave of relief swept over him. He realised that option three had been there all along. True, it had been disguised as option one, but it was definitely option three.

"Do it!" said Hoops. "Crash into it!"

"Are you sure?"

"Definitely. Crash right into that truck."

"Okay," said Clownshoes. "Let's do this!" He turned his attention back to the controls and continued with his dive.

"Only, we won't die," added Hoops.

"I think we will," said Nathalie, "we're about to crash a shuttlecraft into a mining truck on the moon."

"But we won't die, because we're with Clownshoes and he's lucky," said Hoops.

Clownshoes and Nathalie glanced at each other.

"He's not that lucky, Arnopp," said Nathalie.

"It doesn't matter how lucky he is, it just matters that he's lucky. Actually, we're all lucky, mankind is lucky. The fact that we're still here, in 2171, is beyond luck. How did we get this far, how did we dodge the asteroids, the ice ages, the nuclear cold wars? How did we survive the twenty-first century, come to that? There was no way we should have survived that, with runaway climate chaos and ecosystems collapsing left, right and centre, on land and on sea, with the energy crisis and the water crisis and the economic collapse? There was no way we were going to make it through that without living in caves, no way at all. And yet, here we are, on the moon. We're just lucky. We're lucky, lucky bastards and no-one is more of a lucky bastard then Clownshoes Fantastic. So go ahead, crash into it, I think we'll be okay."

"It's a theory," said Nathalie.

Clownshoes shrugged. "Let's put it to the test," he said.

35.

The question of how western civilisation survived the twenty-first century is an interesting one. It is perhaps best summarised by the great French anarchist and thinker Pedwar Tot. Tot memorably described that strange turn in events as "just one of those things, brother, don't hassle me."

In the late twenty-first century, things were very bleak. Plants were extremely confused about what it was they were supposed to be doing. Fish called it a day and decided to pack it in, and the water cycle was, to put it mildly, not helpful. It didn't seem to matter how much economists shouted at the unpredictable weather patterns, the planet's ecosystems still refused to generate sufficient food to feed the human population. The global economy had been a wild, uncontrollable beast ever since oil went over $500 a barrel, and only lunatics went anywhere near it. Politicians and economists had taken to hiding in elaborate underground fortresses, which was something of a blessing for everyone else, but even that did not compensate for the endless wildfires, hurricanes, droughts and general bad vibes. There are only so many thousand bodies you can bury before it starts to get you down.

It was at this point that a blue bottle washed up on the shores of South Korea, containing the blueprints for a small, cheap and mass producible fusion reactor.

Nobody knew where this had come from. All nations and corporations were quizzed, but no-one could take credit because no-one was even close to being able to invent such a marvel. The design had brilliantly solved the problem of plasma instability by an ingenious inversion of the magnetic field strength. As a result the reactor was portable, completely safe and allowed humanity to produce as much clean energy as it wanted. Desalination plants could now produce endless supplies of drinking water. Pumping carbon into the atmosphere became a thing of the past, only practiced by nostalgia enthusiasts for old time's sake.

None of this solved the Earth's problems overnight, of course, and it will still take many generations before the planet's ecosystems reach a level of stability. But for mankind, it was the miracle they needed. They now had hope. Hope is the sort of thing you don't realise is important until after it's gone. There would be a future, so it was worth working towards one. And if the politicians and economists could be trapped underground in their bunkers and not allowed out, then even better. People no longer took the view that the fish had had the right idea, or that it would be better if everyone just gave up.

All of which raised the question of where those plans came from. Jennifer Hammerpot, the Agnostic Bishop of Southwark, had argued that they must have come from the mythical isolated nation of America, and that they should be seen as proof that beneath its mysterious shield the country was still populated. Indeed, it must in fact have been doing quite well. Who else, she asked, would invent such a device? Who else could aim that high and actually manage to pull it off, but the Americans? These were rhetorical questions, and no-one really had an answer to them. People were, by and large, more interested in the fact that the fusion reactors existed than where they came from.

Bishop Hammerpot's theory that the plans were American in origin never gained widespread acceptance, even though one page of the blueprints was smeared with ketchup. This, Jennifer argued, was a total giveaway.

36.

A sixth sense persuaded Marcus to turn. It was not a sound, because there was no sound on the moon. It was not a passing shadow, because the sun was not visible and the light from the Earth was directly in front of him. But something persuaded him to turn, and that's when he saw the shuttle. It was tiny, but growing quickly. It was going to crash, there was no doubt about that. It was coming in far too fast to land. Marcus allowed himself a moment to watch its approach and to come to terms with what he was seeing. Then he turned and bounded out of the way as fast as he damn well could.

Clownshoes, Nathalie and Arnopp Hoops were strapped in tight. Clownshoes was focused on the controls, while Nathalie and Arnopp watched the countdown on the screen above them. This helpfully counted down the seconds to impact in a calming, elegant font.

'8', it said. '7… 6… 5…'

It followed this with a '4'.

Clownshoes gripped the manual controls with total focus. Beads of sweat prickled his forehead. He may have forgotten to breathe at this point, it was hard to tell.

'3'.

Arnopp and Nathalie remained fixed on the countdown screen because this was better than looking out of the window. The window was full of hard rocks approaching at a really worrying speed.

After '3', the screen said '2'.

Clownshoes hiccupped.

He hadn't meant to. It just erupted out of nowhere. It caused his body to jerk, which in turn caused his hands to jerk the joystick back. This was just for a fraction of a second, but that was enough to pull up the nose of the shuttle when as it was mere meters from punching into the truck like a fist into concrete.

The nose of the shuttle missed the body of the truck. It hit the dish on the top directly, causing it to shatter in a shower of metal. The shuttlecraft passed just inches over the truck, over the body of Bishop Hammerpot lying on the Eagle Lander, and finally touched ground perhaps thirty meters beyond them. It shuddered and bounced and scraped along the ground, sending clouds of dust up into the blackness of space. Gradually, it slowed and eventually came to a halt on the lip of a large crater, leaving a long, arcing curve of about half a kilometre in length gauged into the surface of the moon.

For a moment, there was calm. Then the edge of the crater crumbled and the ship toppled in, ending up on its roof like a tormented tortoise.

Inside the ship, Clownshoes, Nathalie and Arnopp dared to breathe again.

They were upside down, strapped into flight seats which now hung down like lampshades on a ceiling. Cautiously, they listened for the hiss of air that would follow a hull breach, but miraculously the shuttle was silent.

Slowly, Nathalie unclipped her harness, and floated down in the low lunar gravity to what had been the roof. She began to check on the integrity of the craft. Clownshoes also headed down, in order to treat himself to a shot of vodka. Hoops stayed where he was, staring straight ahead and remembering to breathe.

Nathalie reassured herself that the shuttle was intact, and that they were in fact safe. She then turned to Clownshoes. "You lucky bastard," she said.

He nodded, and necked the vodka.

Nathalie had an urge to see where they had landed. The upturned ship meant that the flight deck windows were above her head, so she dragged some scattered debris across the flight deck and used it to climb up to the window. Balancing carefully, she peered out at the surface of the moon.

The grey wall of the crater was to her left. It rose up for about ten meters until it was replaced by the blackness of deep space. She scanned the horizon, looking for a way to climb out of the crater.

And then Marcus Milk appeared, on the lip of the crater wall. Even in his heavy environment suit she recognised him immediately. He, in turn, looked down at the crashed shuttle and saw her in the window. He slowly raised a hand, not quite believing what was happening. She raised a hand in response.

Marcus, still acting automatically, held out his other hand and displayed the gold ring clenched in his palm. Even at that distance, the object was unmistakeable. This was a world of grey and silver. There was no mistaking gold.

Nathalie smiled, and held up her left hand to display the matching ring around her thumb.

Meanwhile, the abort command arrived at the three mobile light trucks thanks to the destruction of the transmitting dish. They then cancelled their plans to blast the shuttle out of space. They did this casually and immediately and didn't make a fuss about it.

Later that day, when Arnopp Hoops returned to the moonbase, he took the cat out of the tumble drier.

EPILOGUE

One week later there were three weddings and a funeral on the moon. It was in many ways like the twentieth century movie *Four Weddings And A Funeral*, if that had been reimagined for a generation with a shorter attention span.

The funeral was Bishop Hammerpot's. Now that her role in the historic discovery of the Eagle Lander was understood, it had been decided that a fitting tribute would be to bury her on the Sea of Tranquillity next to the Lander itself. This is what she would have wanted, everyone said. Which was true, apart from the whole 'being dead' bit.

Pope Tom travelled to the moon in order to perform the funeral and the three weddings. This was the first off-world Papal visit in history, and that was one 'first' which did get noted in the history books. His shuttle was equipped, Hoops had been pleased to note, with all the velvet drapes and golden bling the Pope's status required.

For the crew of the Steve Moore Moonbase, Pope Tom's arrival was a cause of great celebration. Even those who had no time for the Agnostic religion were excited, because it wasn't every day you get to beat a

Pope at table tennis. Also, everyone loves a wedding, and weddings officiated by Popes were as good as they got.

The first wedding was something of a surprise. No-one had known when they greeted the Pope's shuttlecraft that he had brought the actress Lily Boop along with him. Ms Boop had decided to accept Commander Milk's proposal and had arrived, with film crew in tow, in order to be moon-wed asap. Gregor was absolutely delighted, and her breasts really did look amazing in low gravity.

This wedding was the first wedding on the moon. It was a huge news story in almost every part of Planet Earth. Most countries were finding the Canadians to be a bit full of themselves at that time, so they were grateful for a distraction.

The second wedding was carried out in secret, on the advice of Pope Tom. This was the shotgun wedding of Dennis and Julie. It followed Julie's shock realisation that he was pregnant. No-one could say how this miracle had happened, least of all Dennis and Julie, who were somewhat freaked out. Nevertheless, a new entity was undoubtedly growing inside Julie's silicon, and no-one could say what it would grow into or how it would develop. Pope Tom knew better than anyone how much trouble virgin births could cause. This was one situation that the Agnostic Church would have to play by ear, he decided, and married them quietly in the computer room during the interval between human weddings.

After that ceremony was complete, Pope Tom spoke privately to Dennis and Julie. They dutifully gave the Pope all the information they had about Orlando Monk's time on the moonbase. The Pope placed this information inside the very old, jewelled and leather-bound papal laptop that he had brought with him for this purpose. This computer dated back to the early twenty-first century. The database it contained had begun with a couple of handwritten pages ripped from a notebook, but it had grown considerably over the decades. Pope Tom concluded his business with Dennis and Julie discreetly, so that nobody would think that this was the actual purpose of his visit.

The third wedding was that of Marcus Milk and Nathalie Grindles. This was the one that everyone was particularly forward to.

The grand moonbase hall was decorated identically to their first wedding attempt, because no one had got round to taking the decorations down. The guests were dressed in the same clothes as before, as few people had a choice of formal wear on the moon. Nathalie's dress didn't look quite as good, having been stretched by Clownshoes Fantastic, but she was in too good a mood to care. Clownshoes had apologised and she had accepted his apology, and also forgiven him for the business with the stationery cupboard. She no longer had any intention of ripping his eyes out. The pair would become firm friends, even though Clownshoes failed to turn up to her wedding. He had been introduced to Doctor Alan and Chef Lark over lunch, and things had got messy.

The ceremony began. Many present thought that Pope Tom's booming voice gave it the edge over Bishop Hammerpot's original version, but they were too respectful of the dead to say so out loud.

The service repeated the first attempt exactly, until it fell to Nathalie Grindles to say "I do."

At that point, Nathalie fell silent.

Nathalie looked at the floor, and the moment stretched out longer than anyone in the audience could bear.

Awkward glances flashed around the room. There was no-one present who wasn't either giving or receiving an awkward glance. Marcus looked like his eyes were going to fall out.

She Nathalie collapsed into laughter, because who could resist pulling that gag in the circumstances? And she declared loudly, "I do!", and hugged and kissed her new husband to great cheers and applause. Marcus was in a state of sheer ecstasy, for a declaration like that means a lot in a period where free will exists, and also because he was still a bit strange following his time looking at the Earth.

At that point the lights on twelve mobile light trucks flared into brilliant illumination, and the entire population of Europe, Africa and Asia looked up to see a heart outlined on the moon.

This broke many regulations, but nobody minded because it really was a very lovely thing.

Next:

Phwoar & Peace

BY THE SAME AUTHOR:

THE BRANDY OF THE DAMNED

Russell, Penny and Will have not seen each other for twenty years. Why, then, do they spend a month driving around the coast of Britain in a van refusing to listen to music? Why do they find little blue bottles washing up on the shore containing pages from a future Bible? And why is Penny carrying such a huge spade?

Funny, surprising and good-hearted, The Brandy of the Damned is a dream-like short novel that leaves the reader strangely grounded and which reveals different things each time it is read. It is the literary equivalent of stepping off the path and heading out into the woods, knowing that if you can't see what's ahead you are never bored. The Brandy of the Damned is a genuinely original story told by a unique voice

(P) The Big Hand 2012
ISBN 978-0956416353
Available on ebook and paperback.

THE KLF: CHAOS, MAGIC AND THE BAND WHO BURNED A MILLION POUNDS

They were the best-selling singles band in the world. They had awards, credibility, commercial success and creative freedom.

They then deleted their records, erased themselves from musical history and burnt their last million pounds in a boathouse on the Isle of Jura.

But they couldn't say why.

This is the story of The KLF, told through the ideas that drove them. It is a story about Carl Jung, Alan Moore, Robert Anton Wilson, Ken Campbell, Dada, Situationism, Discordianism, magic, chaos, punk, rave and the alchemical symbolism of Doctor Who.

Wildly unauthorised and unlike any other music biography, this is a trawl through chaos on a hunt for meaning.

(P) Phoenix 2013
ISBN 978-1780226552
Available on ebook and paperback.

I HAVE AMERICA SURROUNDED: THE LIFE OF TIMOTHY LEARY

Timothy Leary was one of the most controversial and divisive figures of the twentieth century. President Nixon called him 'the most dangerous man in America.' Hunter S. Thompson said that he was 'not just wrong, but a treacherous creep and a horrible goddamn person.' Yet the writer Terence McKenna claims that he 'probably made more people happy than anyone else in history.'

A brilliant Harvard psychologist, Leary was sacked because of his research into LSD and other psychedelic drugs. He went on to become the global figurehead of the 1960s drug culture, coin the phrase 'tune in, turn on and drop out', and persuade millions of people to take drugs and explore alternative lifestyles yet the tremendous impact of his 'scandalous' research has been so controversial that it has completely overshadowed the man himself and the details of his life. Few people realise that Timothy Leary's life is one of the greatest untold adventure stories of the twentieth century.

Timothy Leary led a life of unflagging optimism and reckless devotion to freedom. It was, in the words of his goddaughter Winona Ryder, 'not just epic grandeur but flat-out epic grandeur.' Leary's life is undoubtedly one of the greatest untold adventure

stories of the twentieth century and this book presents
it for the first time in all its uncensored glory.

(P) THE FRIDAY PROJECT 2006
ISBN 978-1905548255
Available on ebook and paperback.

THANKS

Huge thanks to the following for their comments and reactions to early drafts, and for pointing out typos and flagging up the unfunny bits:

Matt Tiller, Shardcore, Joanne Mallon, Chris Stone, Zenbullets, Gary Acord, Tom Jackson, Hector Monk MP, Scott Pack and Jason Arnopp.

CPSIA information can be obtained
at www.ICGtesting.com
Printed in the USA
BVHW080324020822
643541BV00010B/1204

9 780956 416339